Ron Mueller

❧ *The Future Awaits* ☙
By Ron Mueller

Around the World Publishing LLC
Cincinnati, Ohio

The Future Awaits ©

Ron Mueller

All rights reserved, including the right of reproduction, in whole or in part in any form. This story is a work of fiction. Names, characters, places, and incidents either are products of the author's imagination or are used fictitiously. Any resemblance to actual events or locales or persons, living or dead, is entirely coincidental.

Distributed by Ingram
ISBN 13: 978-1-68223-220-0

Distributed by Ingram
Cover Design by Ron Mueller
Picture by Kevin Carden, Dreamstime.com

The Future Awaits

1 Synchronization

Distant Future

E mma was out celebrating her one hundred seventh birthday. In another three years she would officially cross into middle age. She was beginning to wonder if living longer was all that great. She was leading the extraction of people from some five hundred years ago so they could be processed and then sent back to an ancient time. The goal was to bolster the currently failing human DNA by strengthening the DNA early in the development of the human species.

She often joked about the ability of scientists being able to extend life but failing to learn how to maintain the health of the fundamental building blocks that made humans human.

Her team had learned how to manipulate time by folding space. She and a team had developed the mathematics that defined how space and time could be folded and manipulated. In essence they had learned to create the fold.

1

They could capture objects from the past if the objects were at the exact point of the fold.

Positioning the physical extraction unit to an exact fold position of the object to be extracted turned out to be a major extraction obstacle. They had not figured out how to move the target object to them, they had to physically be at the exact extraction site at the moment of capture.

Emma had lost count of the number of failures of positioning their equipment at exactly the right physical position.

She had become, anthropologist, cartographer, and an expert in dynamic topography in her attempts at accurately positioning her equipment.

Five hundred years of topographic and positional change needed to be exactly understood and compensating adjustments made.

Once she focused on the historic events that got detailed news reporting and coverage her extraction success rate went up dramatically. These were most often catastrophic events in large cities.

Getting her first extraction was dramatic for the extraction effort.

Her extractions were still crude. Their extracted subjects all suffered fresh bone fractures when they appeared in the extraction landing area

Once these subjects were healed, they were reinserted into the past.

The success of their six re-insertions were unconfirmed. They had no way knowing.

Their only check on their success was to monitor the condition of the Human DNA and determine if there was any improvement. So far, she and the team had not been able to see a single improvement.

Emma concluded that the cycle of extraction, reinsertion and then seeing if the DNA history improved was a million was a times worse than looking for a needle in a haystack.

She was looking for a breakthrough.

Emma walked through the extraction unit in historic downtown New York City. She and her team were on the ninety fifth floor of the Great American Tower. It was the location where American Flight 11 crashed into the North Tower of The World Trade Center. Their goal was to extract the three people sitting in coach in the first row of the right-hand side exit windows.

The unit was as accurately placed as Emma could ascertain the exact location of the plane, and the seats. She hoped the details she had gleaned from months working with her team to determine the exact position of the three were accurate.

She had spent weeks negotiating the access and use of the space. The owner and renters were co-operative once they learned she had the right of eminent domain. She had spent extra time educating them and, in the end, they were very co-operative. They made a point of highlighting the cooperation to the press. Emma threw in a good word for them.

Current Time

Adam was the product of working hard for his father on their ranch, playing hard on the slopes of Grand Targhee Ski resort and of studying hard because he was hooked on learning.

His Dad used hard work as a way to instill what he called "character and excellence." By character, his Dad meant honesty, integrity, and respect for all individuals and the will to achieve. By excellence, his Dad meant doing your best at what you set out to do and later looking back and figuring out how to do better.

His Dad and he had gone through scouting together. His Dad led the Cub Scout Pack. Later they both progressed together to a Troop his Dad led. Hiking the many trails through the Teton was a summer event for the Troop. Adam's Eagle Scout project was to create a map of the hiking trails and to create connecting trails to create a new trail from Alta across the Tetons to Jackson Hole.

Adam and his team of about twenty scouts spent almost two years in connecting and mapping thirty-five miles between Alta and Jackson Hole Wyoming, through the Teton mountain range.

Adam's mother simplified her teaching to a simple phrase "treat others the way you wish to be treated." She was always there to support Adam.

Loving his parents, learning from them, growing up on the ranch. What more could he want?

He worked at school hard as or harder than he worked on the ranch. School was a treat for him. He did not care for sports and his Dad did not push him in this area. Adam fell in love with the history of the Greeks and Romans.

The details of Alexander the Great's travels and battles were all played out when he rode his horse around the ranch or through the mountains. The fact that Alexander had accomplished this in the years before he died at the age of thirty-three made Adam feel like an underachiever.

He graduated from Teton High in Driggs, Idaho at the top of his class and was accepted into MIT where he studied Mechanical Engineering.

Adam was hooked on history, hooked on the evolution of technology, hooked on how equipment and machinery transitioned from early and almost useless innovation like the engine to sophisticated power plants that provided the world with electricity.

The best vacation he had ever taken was the tour of the Henry Ford Museum in Detroit with his Mom and Dad over an entire spring break. The transition of the technological transition from an early invention into the modern and useful tool was fascinating to him.

In the MIT laboratory he proved he could make the common slant six engine achieve fifty miles to the gallon. He wondered about the fact that if he could do it, why the big three had not done it.

Four years and graduation came much too fast. The job interviews were discouraging. The jobs seemed to go from just acceptable to really boring. He received three very good salary offers that would have been financially lucrative, but they all seemed boring.

His Dad rescued him when he asked him to help out on running the Horn family Ranch.

Working the ranch and not having any schoolwork was a refreshing experience. His skiing skills improved dramatically. Junior his horse and he traveled new trails and fished new streams for trout every weekend.

One day Junior faltered. Adam realized that Junior was now no longer junior. Adam put Junior out to pasture with the other horses. Junior would have a few more good years, but time had caught up.

Adam suddenly became acutely aware that time was passing, and he had not accomplished any of the things in his earlier dreams.

Involvement in the details of running the ranch had given him an appreciation for the financial and business acumen needed to be successful. He became more impressed with his parents capability.

He decided that he would get a master's degree in either finance or business administration. He took a GMAT preparation class offered at Teton High.

He did fairly well. He was at the top end of the top tenth percentile.

He decided to aim as high as he could and applied at Harvard, Yale, Dartmouth, Stanford, Brown, and Columbia.

He was surprised to get accepted at Stanford and Dartmouth.

Adam selected Stanford, during his jog of the wide-open campus with its buildings set purposely far apart, and the sunny pleasant seventy-degree weather, spiced by the roller blading long legged young women. He was sure he would get a good education as well.

The business courses seemed unusually simple to him. He often walked out of class with his homework done.

He spent more time in the Gym than on his class work.

He tried the beach scene, but the water was cold and laying on a towel in the sun did not attract him.

He realized one morning his time at the university was almost at an end. He needed to make a critical decision.

What was he going to do with his life? It was interview time.

The graduate support office posted the company interview schedule. The postings did not inspire him. Dull, Dull, Dull, Dull, seemed to follow his reading of each company description. Ranch life was beginning to look better all the time.

None the less he prepared a resume. He studied each company to understand their business. Several of the larger companies offered management development programs with six-month assignments to three or four parts of their business. These were the ones Adam applied to interview. He hoped he would find a home in some part of their business.

His lack of interest must have come through in his interviews. Only one company made him an offer.

He of course accepted but negotiated a start date six months in the future.

He decided to take his Dad up on the advice to see the world before starting to work.

The Horn Ranch trust fund, as his Dad called the family ranch, would pay the way.

Adam spent a month in Asia. He spent a week each in Japan, Korea, China, Thailand, and Cambodia.

In Cambodia he spent a week in the Angkor Watt region. This was a piece of history never covered in his history studies. He had accidently discovered the Angkor site when researching his round-the-world trip.

The region was huge and the number of temples, dating back before the Greek and Roman Empires, were so numerous he wondered how historians had overlooked such an immense and long-lived empire.

He then went to India to see the Taj Mahal. This was a tomb built to commemorate love. He stood for a long time looking at this tomb wondering about the details of a love affair that could lead to such a symbol.

His stops in Europe include Turkey, Greece, Italy, Spain, France, and England. He spent two weeks in each country.

Each yielded yet more ammunition to a mounting sense of his under-achievement.

He now watched the Coast of New York come into view as he landed at La Guardia. He had gone around the world and was now going home before starting his working career.

He was slowly recalling the last few months as he watched the Coast of New York come into view. The plane was landing at La Guardia.

Adam had gone around the world and was now returning to the ranch before starting his working career.

Adam walked to the gate where his flight to Idaho Falls was scheduled to depart. He had been able to get an emergency exit seat but had to settle for a middle seat.

He was the first of the three and sat down but left his seat belt hanging loose.

He watched and tried to guess who would sit next to him.

Hanna had rushed back to LaGuardia to make her flight back to the west coast. She had stayed with a friend in Harford and together they had participated in the Harford Marathon. The two had finished in the main body of participants and were happy with their showing.

They then participated in the Monster Trail Marathon held in Virgil, New York.

Two Marathon in two weeks had been a challenge they had shared with each other in their senior year together at the University of Washington.

She had trained long and hard. She had run strong. She felt great about the results.

Hanna looked back at her academic experience and realized that it was the environment that provided her the transition, from being the daughter of a successful charter fisherman, as she fondly thought of her parents, to realizing her own success in the same field.

Hanna now managed an all-female run and staffed charter fishing boat she had purchased, reconditioned, and renamed, *"Big Fish."*

Her best friend Cathy, now residing on the east coast, ran the financial and advertising side of the business. Cathy had developed an advertising campaign using a handsome muscular bare chested male model and some scantily clad female models. The advertising blurb was, *we bait, we hook, we catch,* "Big Fish"

The crew V cut T shirts had the words, *"Big Fish"* across the front and the picture of a big fish on the back.

Several roadside billboards with the same picture, a few local and selected TV ads, some local radio spots, and conversations on twitter and U-tube completed the advertising campaign.

Her fishing charter business was an immediate success.

Her boat was constantly full of young attractive men.

Her reservations were full through the entire summer into the fall.

Her crew members were very happy and split a significant tip jar after every cruise.

The fact her boat was twice as productive as her parents became the family joke.

"The guy's come fishing but not for fish," her father accused her.

Hanna laughed, agreed, and wondered about the gullibility of the other sex.

Cathy contacted her with the dual marathon challenge at Christmas. From January to June, Hannah entered three local Marathons.

When August came, she was ready for the double.

The summer fishing had been very lucrative. It was not the best time to leave but she got the previous owner of the *Big Fish* to act as captain for a month.

This allowed her to go for the month to get ready for the double marathon.

She had gotten the emergency row and felt lucky to have the extra room. None the less it was going to be a long trip back to the west coast.

She looked enviously at the first-class seats and wished she had paid to sit up front. She could afford it, but it seemed so excessive to her.

She found it hard to let go of the money she was at last earning.

When she located her seat, she realized she would be sitting next to a rather handsome guy. She hoped he was single and a good conversationalist. It would be great to meet someone she might want to date.

She smiled at him and said hello as he stood to let her get to her window seat.

His reply was a simple Howdy.

Her hopes sank. She was of the opinion that cowboys never talked very much because cows can't talk.

Hanna rescinded herself to a long, quite flight.

Eva Wilkerson walked confidently on to the plane. She was on her way to Alaska for her first true vacation.

She was a Boston, Bean Town, subway rat.

She was in the seventy fifth percentile in her high school class. To her amazement she had received a scholarship to Brown University based on the articles she had written about her travel to every stop on every line of the Boston Subway system.

These articles were printed by the Boston Globe on a or a weekly basis.

Eva found her inner self at Brown. She took up Tae Kwon Do and it became a passion. The concentration and focus she learned in Tae Kwon Do carried over into her classroom work. She soon was recognized for achievements in both areas. She zoomed to the top of her class in both camps.

In her campaign for class president that was focused on individual responsibility, she sparred with individuals labeled with the election issues. She won each match, and she won the election as well.

She was elected by a landslide.

In four years, she earned her bachelor's degree in business and achieved Black Belt status.

She surprised herself by accepting a job at Victoria Secrets as a purchasing agent.

Every time she thought about her career choice a smile would come to her. She was perfectly matched for the challenge of all the jerks who thought women were meant to be in skimpy bras and panties. She knew she could kick their butt.

She secretly liked these skimpy outfits but had never found the right guy to really make them useful.

She was geared for success and was moving successfully up in the Victoria Secrets organization.

The years were now beginning to take their emotional dues. She had not found Mr. Right and she was not sure she would find him anytime soon. She had just dropped her latest Mr. Right, as he went wrong.

None the less, she had a swagger and high energy to her walk. She had just competed in and taken first place in a Tae Kwon Do tournament. At five foot four, she was the smallest competitor and had overcome her much bigger and often stronger but slower rivals.

Her mantra that she repeated before every competition was, "I am tall, I am strong, I am fast. Tall, strong, fast. Tall, strong, fast."

As a head buyer for her company, she had racked up enough miles to be in the Executive Platinum status.

14

She was disappointed that she had only been able to score an aisle seat in the emergency exit row.

She told herself to relax and begin enjoying her vacation.

She was only a few rows away from her seat before she was able to see the other two passengers in her row.

She immediately perked up when she saw the guy with sandy colored hair sitting in the center seat.

Eva immediately wondered if he was single.

She would find out.

Eva looked at the rather good-looking woman sitting by the window.

She offered to take the middle seat but was turned down by Mr. Sandy hair with deep blue eyes.

His cowboy crawl came softly through a strong solid voice and his smile pleased her.

He was definitely not her type. But then she had failed with the ones she that she thought were her type. It probably didn't matter.

It would be a long flight to Salt Lake. She would learn what she could about Mr. Sandy hair.

Distant Future

Emma finished her inspection tour. She had nothing pressing to do and decided to catch a play on Broadway as a way to distract herself. She exited the building and walked through the park. The never cut grass was at the chosen height of four inches.

A circular display of Asters with their yellow trimmed red petals open like a broad flat beach umbrella with a deep red puff caused her to pause. They cheered her up and yet made her sad.

A small black hummingbird, just slightly larger than a large bumble bee, with a red chest trimmed in yellow guided her eyes to some horned like lavender flowers. Each stem had multiple horns. The small hummingbird briefly visited each blossom in bottom to top order.

The hummingbird and his precision in hovering, extracting the nectar made her think about the location precision and the 8:46:40 am time precision that needed to occur across five hundred years.

2 Extraction

The future

mma had no trouble getting up. After the show she decided to take a cab back to the Marriot. She hoped she could get a couple of hours sleep before returning to the extraction site.

That hope did not materialize. She lay in the dark thinking through every detail leading up to and the rehabilitation of the three after the extraction.

Emma had spent years studying the horrific details of the terrorist destruction of the Twin Towers of the world trade center. She had the timing of events down to the hundredth of a second. She had the elevation down to one hundredth of an inch.

This was not the first extraction, but it would test the limits at how fast they could carry out an extraction. The targeted three would approach the extraction point at four hundred sixty-six mile per hour or 683.466667 feet per second.

The extraction would require the system to transfer the three subjects as they went past a transfer plane less than one hundredth of a second thick.

The power draw would be enormous. Most of the cost for this extraction had been to the electrical power company to run special cabling and deliver the power to the extraction unit. Emma had considered extracting only one but that proved to be technically more difficult, so she and the team had come to the agreement to extract all three.

Emma and her team had practiced this transfer speed with a glob of organic material that was as close to simulating a human as they could devise. They did it successfully seven times.

She was still not satisfied. She had a huge concern about retrieving live humans.

Current Time

Adam watched as, first one very attractive brunette sat down beside him on the window side and then a petite well, built blond took the aisle seat. He was sitting between two very good-looking ladies.

He decided it was his lucky day. The final leg of his trip might be the best part of the trip. How was he going to handle two good looking women sitting next to him?

He recalled his Dad's saying, "Stopping stampeding cattle is an easier job then dealing with women."

He was now looking forward to the Flight to LA.

The flight attendant verified their willingness to operate the safety door as the plane prepared to leave the gate.

He started with a self-introduction and that he was going home to Idaho when the take-off delay was announced.

Hanna surprised the cowboy was talking, so she shared her recent Marathon experience and that she was returning to Seattle.

Eva was surprised at herself when she admitted dumping her most recent boyfriend but still taking her planned vacation to Alaska on her own. Mr. Sandy hair, Adam, was having a disarming effect on her.

Emma, some five hundred years in the future, was anxiously watching the count-down clock. In spite of the grumbling of her team, she once again made them check out all the systems and every detail of the extraction process

Emma watched the big screen as it detailed the events happening to American Flight 11 on a second-by-second basis. The computer was in control of the extraction. It would trigger the extraction at the precise millisecond.

She was mentally living through the events experienced by Eva, Adam, and Hanna. She was the fourth passenger sitting with them. She saw the plane turn into a fireball before her eyes. Her emotions were raw as she hypnotically watched the computer count down the time in an excruciatingly slow pace.

The extraction flash startled her, and the team went into the extraction delay time.

Current to Future

The Statue of Liberty came into sight. Adam realized that the hijackers were not landing at Logan. They were not returning to the airport.

Both Hanna and Eva were holding his hand. He looked at each of them and saw tears in their eyes. He squeezed their hands.

Suddenly a terrific impact slammed him forward. He hit his head on his knees.

He saw the flames engulfing the plane.

There would be no escape.

They were dead.

He was still holding their hands. It was pitch black, but he could see that they were nude. He looked for burn marks, but they had none. Both Hanna and Eva were out.

Totally confused he saw a bright white light ahead. He pulled both of them to him and realized they felt cold.

He was embracing two naked young women. What a weird way to experience death.

The white light was rushing toward him at a high speed. At the last moment as he reached the light he instinctively spun around.

The last thing he remembered was the impact as they hit the white light.

He slowly opened his eyes. The room he was in was dark and empty. He didn't feel dead but how would he know what death felt like. He realized that the mattress had shaped itself to his body. He felt comfortable and warm.

He tried to talk to the grey haired, grey bearded old man in a white lab coat that reminded him of a white bearded Abraham Lincoln.

Emma stepped around Lincoln and found herself looking directly into Adam's deep blue eyes. None of the extraction subjects had ever awakened during their stay in this time period. Her partner immediately instructed the system to give the patient another shot of the sedative.

He tried to argue but he could not get his voice to activate. He was slowly drifting away. He heard the young slender woman with piercing green eyes and jet-black hair telling a Dr. Orenski that he should have consulted her before ordering additional sedatives.

Adam could hear the Dr. reply that their three subjects should not know anything about this time. They should remain unconscious until reinsertion.

His world was slowly going black, but he was still thinking and he fought to stay awake.

The Dr. had mentioned three subjects.

Did he mean Hanna and Eva?

Was his trip down the tunnel to the light real?

Where was he and in what time?

For a moment, he saw the log framed gate to the Horn ranch. He and his father had made a trip to the lumber yard with their flatbed truck to select the six logs with which to make the gate. Each log was eighteen inches in diameter. The four vertical logs were each twenty-four feet long and the two horizontal logs were thirty-two feet long.

They had worked for almost a week to sink and anchor the vertical logs and put the crossing ones on top.

He spent two days sealing and varnishing the entire structure.

His mind locked on this memory and his body responded with a surge of new energy.

He got mad. He was not in bandages and did not feel mutilated or burned as he expected to be. He willed himself awake. He opened his eyes and looked around his dark empty room.

He was groggy and wobbly but otherwise he actually felt rested. He looked down at his naked body. He was in great shape and kept himself that way by doing a minimum of five hundred sit ups a day, doing his Tae Kwon Do exercises and getting in a three-to-five-mile jog three times a week. He sported a solid six pack on a one hundred-and-seventy-two-pound, six-foot two frame.

He wrapped the single sheet from the bed around his waist.

He and the bed were the only two objects in the room. He walked to the door and realized he did not know how to open it. It felt solid to the touch of his hand.

His instinct caused him to push the bed toward the door. Instead of the impact he had prepared for, the bed just passed through. He stopped the bed when it was half-of-the-way through and crawled out underneath it.

He then pulled the bed the rest of the way out into the hallway and parked it by the wall next to the door beneath a window that seemed to look into his room.

He walked to his right and peered into the window of the room next to his. The room was dark but slowly his eyes made out the figure of Hanna laying beneath a sheet. He walked to the next window and found Eva.

They were both out.

He decided to continue down the hallway.

Several windows later he looked into a room that looked like a scientific laboratory. The door blocked his entrance.

He returned and retrieved his bed and was pleasantly surprised when it passed through the doorway and he was able to crawl underneath into the lab.

By examining the door more carefully, Adam realized that it must be some sort of force field. The bed was in the program and, evidently, he was not.

Since he was able to use the bed in the manner that he was doing, he gave the programmer a D in programing. Adam took comfort that the human mind still had its blind spots.

The lab, as he thought about the room, was devoid of the lab equipment that he would have expected in his time. Adam had no idea how and what kinds of experiments would be done in this time period or what a lab equipment would look.

He walked over to the only counter that had anything physical on it.

He picked up the instrument and turned it over. The label date was twenty-five-sixty-seven.

He let the date sink in.

Now he knew that he was more than five hundred years into the future.

Adam walked across the room to a box sitting on a table. "Molecular Blades, Handle with Care" was stenciled in red across the top of the box.

He followed instructions and carefully opened the lid. He peered down at six thin long blades that reminded him of his prized hunting knife. These seemed to be ceramic with the sharp edge on both sides.

He had never seen anything look this sharp.

Adam took the edge of the bed sheet he was wearing and let it fall on one of the blades. He pulled the bed sheet along the blade and was amazed when the blade cut easily through. These blades were sharp beyond anything he had ever imagine.

He instinctively knew these blades were valuable in the situation he found himself. He took the box and placed it on the shelf beneath his bed. The box was not visible to a standing observer.

It was time to get back to his room.

He had just made it back and gotten into his bed when he heard someone talking.

He immediately closed his eyes and began a slow steady breathing rhythm.

The technician was claiming that there was something wrong with the vision system. Adam could hear Dr. Jekyll as Adam was now thinking of him, telling the technician to get things checked out.

Adam strained to hear the conversation between Ms. Green Eyes and Dr. Jekyll as they stood outside his door and discussed the upcoming reinsertion scheduled in two days.

Their three subjects would be reinserted in sequence as rapidly as the system could recharged to handle the transmissions. It was their hope that the three would arrive close together in the same time period.

Ms. Green Eyes closed by saying that Adam would be sent first in hopes that's he would survive to help the other two.

Adam was now putting all the pieces together. He was sure he; Eva and Hanna were listed as dead in their time.

They had somehow been pulled from the burning plane wreck and brought into the future. The three were being conditioned to be sent back in time.

As he continued to listen, he became aware that the three of them were a part of an experiment in improving the human intelligence by improving the DNA strain far back into the past.

He learned that part of the conditioning they were currently receiving was to increase their life span and to make their bodies more tolerant to cold.

They had also been programed with survival skills.

Adam almost let out a chuckle when he realized he was just an experiment for a group of mad scientists.

Adam was sure he was now being watched. He almost let out a cheer when the room went totally dark.

He moved his hands around above him and was relieved when nothing happened.

He got out of his bed and pushed his bed through the door. He entered into Hanna's room and tried to wake her. She stayed out cold. He had the same experience with Eva.

He immediately went to the lab where he found yet another box.

He opened this smaller box to find three knives made of the same material as the other blades he had already allocated. Adam thought allocated sounded so much better than stealing.

He looked at the set of blades and came to the realization that one set of blades seemed designed to become spearheads and the knives in the new box were meant to be hunting knives

He "allocated" the box with the knives and put them next to the box of spear heads.

He returned to the hallway and was about to go back to his room when he was attracted to the light coming from the room labeled Extraction-Reinsertion. He looked in through the window and was surprised to see several people sitting looking at what seemed to be a holographic control panel.

He immediately ducked down and hurriedly pushed his bed back to his room. He got back into his bed and immediately fell asleep.

He came immediately awake when he heard Dr. Jekyll's voice. Who referred to Ms. Green Eyes as Emma and was still arguing about keeping the subjects asleep in their time period. He was arguing that being sent back thirty thousand years, after experiencing the wonders of this time period, would be demoralizing.

An almost electric shock went through him as Emma, with the penetrating green eyes and jet-black hair was asking why they were re-inserting the three into the Yellow Stone.

Dr. Jekyll explained that it was the only location that would lock in and hold. The other locations in Europe and Africa were for some reason intermittent.

I think the future is limiting our choices, Adam heard Dr. Jekyll speculate.

Emma and Dr. Jekyll walked away discussing how the future could influence what they did now that they had invented the ability to manipulate the space time continuum.

Adam was glad he was flat in his bed as he listened. He was actually wishing he hadn't heard the discussion.

Going back to the Yellow Stone thirty thousand years in the past sounded more appealing. In this time period and the ever-onward reality would always be at the mercy of the upstream time period. History from this point on would always be changed based on the upstream need.

Adam's Boy Scout experience gave him confidence in his ability to survive. He knew how; to make fire, to create an oven to bake in and how to make a fishhook with which to fish.

He began thinking through all of his outdoor survival skills. Living in the wild did not bother him as much as the future these people would have to live through.

He knew the mountains of the Yellow Stone Rockies.

Sometime on the following day was re-insertion. Adam relaxed. He wanted to get some asleep. He wanted to do another reconnaissance of the facility this evening.

Adam fell asleep thinking about what else he might be able to find to take back to give him an edge

3 Re-Insertion

mma was feeling flush.

Her team had extracted three people.

They had reconditioned their bodies and extended their lifespan significantly.

They had pumped their brains full of survival knowledge from hunting and shelter building to first aid and fundamental medical training.

Her one disappointment was when Dr. Orenski reported that the special knives and spear heads had not arrived, or they were lost somewhere in the facility.

Dr. Orenski made the point that perhaps the future did not want this to happen.

Adam listened to the conversation between Dr. Orenski and Emma. He wished the trip to the reinsertion room would last long enough for him to learn more.

When the bed stopped moving, Adam chanced a quick look. He saw a square bench or low table in what appeared to be a spotlight and figured that it was the reinsertion point.

Adam decided that surprise would be the weapon of choice. He sprang out of his bed, gave a Tarzan like yell, retrieved his two boxes of blades, and jump into the spotlight.

Adam noticed that everyone seemed frozen where they stood. In a loud voice he let them know he was OK with being sent back in time.

In spite of this one glitch, she had chosen to maintain her re-insertion schedule. Emma did not believe the future would be paying attention to such small details.

He asked if he was landing in Yellow Stone in summer or winter.

Emma replied that there was no way for them to know.

She pointed to the boxes and smiled.

She wondered how Adam had gotten to the knives and spearheads.

She was already thinking that this would be a successful reinsertion.

Emma wished him good luck and then quietly pointed to a person sitting in front of a holographic screen and simply said "Reinsert."

Adam winked out of their presence.

She walked out of the room with tears in her eyes. She knew she had missed a huge opportunity by not having interviewed Adam while he was in her care.

It would not happen again.

Adam was in the dark tunnel once again. He was experiencing a falling sensation. Once again, he felt the disorientation and then he saw a white light.

He immediately recalled his last experience with the white light. He knew there was no control room or landing pad at this end of time.

Then he saw an evergreen tree and the twenty-foot-deep hole of snow it was standing in.

Winter!

Winter was the season into which he was arriving.

He moved as far to the right as he could as he reached the exit from the time tunnel. He was trying not to crash into the pine tree but hit the edge of the snow bowl.

He knew immediately that he was coming in from a height of about forty feet and would hit the snow in an explosive way.

He threw his boxes toward the pine and then gripped the back of his neck with both hands as he went head and elbows into the snow.

He felt the snow give way and swallow him. He was in danger of suffocating. He extended his left arm toward where he thought the pine tree would be.

His hand extended out of the snow.

He slowly rotated his arm and opened a tunnel allowing him to take a deep breath of air.

He slowly worked is other arm toward the opening made by his left hand. He paused periodically as he moved his body toward the pine tree.

He finally was able to slide through the hole and land at the base of the pine tree.

He was sitting on a thick layer of pine needles. One of the boxes was on the ground and the other was up about ten feet caught in the branches of the tree.

He recalled falling into a similar hole while skiing in the Grand Tetons. It had taken him several hours get back out of the hole by using his ski's to step back up out of the bowl.

This time he would need to create some foot gear to get out. This time he was totally nude and would need to utilize his knife set to cut and create what he needed.

He was feeling cold and knew that getting to shelter and warmth was of critical importance.

The knives were wonderful tools. He was able to cut the half inch limbs with ease. He soon had some ski like snowshoes about three feet long. He took five half inch branches and tied them together with bark strips from branches, to make some snowshoes.

After cutting one larger limb he took one of the spearheads and bound it into the slot created by splitting the end of the limb.

He looked up the twenty-foot side of the bowl he was in and began to slowly climb out. He began by placing the two boxes into the snow as high as he could reach. Then he kicked the snowshoe halfway into the side the snow and lifted himself up to that level. He then did the same with his other foot.

When the boxes were at waist level. He punched his left arm all the way into the snow and with his right arm he moved the boxes above his head and push them into the snow.

He let out a triumphant yell when several hours later he threw the two boxes up out of the bowl and pulled himself over the top edge.

He would need to be back at this point when Hanna and Eva came through. He was standing looking down a steep slope. The terrain went up to what seemed to be a mountain behind him. Should he go left, right, or down?

He didn't want to go farther up but looked that way to get oriented.

He was glad he did. If down was six o-clock and up was twelve, then at the ten o-clock position was what appeared to be a cave.

He made his way toward the cave. The snowshoes proved to be needed for the hike up to the cave. He carried the extra knives and spearheads with him.

He reached the cave and made his way inside. The cave seemed to narrow toward the back and then opened again.

A shiver went through him. He knew the cave. He had been in it on one of his Boy Scout camping trips. It was the Bear Cave where two giant brown bear skulls had been discovered.

He knew instinctively what he would now find in the back of the cave. He quietly looked through the opening to the back part of the cave. There were two hibernating brown bears. These bears were bigger than the grizzly bear.

He had a spear.

He let his eyes adjust to the light. One bear was laying on its side the other was on its back. He hoped his bear anatomy was accurate. He needed to cut through their hearts and then immediately exit the cave.

He checked the work on his spear.

It was solid.

He quietly approached the first bear. The spear cut in and across with ease. He didn't wait to see how successful he had been but proceeded to immediately do the same with the second bear.

He then ran out as the first bear started to snort.

At the mouth of the cave, he surprised a pack of dire wolves. Each of the wolves was at least four foot high at the shoulders

He proceeded toward them swinging his spear back and forth and shouting curses at them. The pack backed away, but it was clear they were not going to leave.

The rocks around the opening of the cave gave him an idea.

He kept his spear within reach but began to build up a wall to block the opening of the cave. An old dead cedar tree provided the bars to go to the top of the wall of the cave opening.

No bears were coming out after him, so he figured he had successfully killed them while they slept.

He knew it was not a fair fight, but he was now trying to survive.

He gathered all the dead wood around the mouth of the cave and piled it inside. The bears represented a huge survival fortune. They assured survival until spring.

The wolves outside were the biggest survival challenge. They seemed to be bold and unafraid of him.

He remembered the trail out and to the right going along a very steep drop down.

In the morning, he planned to take the entrails from one of the bears and throw it down the grade.

The wolves posed a serious threat to his ability to rescue Hanna and Eva.

He needed time to safely retrieve the two of them. He hoped the two would come through awake.

Adam reassured himself that the wolves could not get into the cave.

He took his knife and went into the back of the cave where the two bears lay dead. He skinned both of them but left them on their skins.

He cut a large circle of hide. He carefully shaved all the hair from the hide. He then carefully cut holes about two inches apart and about one inch in from the edge of the circle.

He shaved the hair from a long piece of hide about one inch wide and three feet long.

Next, he folded the long strip of hide and passed it in and out of the holes in the circular hide. Adam admired his first survival container. He was now prepared to cook his first soup.

He returned to the front of the cave and arranged stones into a cooking ring. He filled the bag with snow and hung it from a branch cut from the tree blocking the cave, held up by a pile of stone.

Next he started a fire. He thought of his Dad who had taught him the technique of twirling a stick placed on a dry piece of wood with fine wood shavings piled generously around. He thanked his Dad as he added small twigs and then larger limbs.

He put round fist sized stones in the center of the fire. Once they were hot, he used a stick with a Y prong at the end and second stick to hold the rock in the prong to pick up the hot stones and drop it into the bag of snow.

Soon he was adding small pieces of meat to the steaming hot water that filled the bag three quarters full. It was then he remembered the pile of salt that was located in the very back of the cave.

He ventured back and found it exactly where it would be in the future when he would first see it.

The aroma of the steaming bear soup had his's stomach growling. He suddenly realized that he did not know how he was going to get the soup from the bag to his mouth.

He inventoried all the resources available to him at the moment. Only one idea came to mind.

Adam returned to the back of the cave and examined the claws of the two bears. Each claw was about the size of the horns of a large male goat. They were close to an inch and half in diameter at their base.

He cut off three of the claws and carried them to the front of the cave where he hollowed them out. He wiped them clean and then dropped them into the hot soup. A few moments later he retrieved them and cleaned their insides again.

He then used one of them to scoop up some the soup and satisfy his hunger. He smiled and complemented himself on the great taste.

The small fire at the mouth of the cave had died down and all Adam could see were a few red coals beneath a thin grey layer of ash.

He put the second notch into the stick on which he was keeping time.

He walked over and stirred the coals before adding a few fresh pieces of wood. It was a dark moonless night and dawn was yet sometime away.

The thought of having to deal with the pack of dire wolves made him nervous and was most likely the reason he was awake so early.

The path outside the cave was much narrower than some thirty thousand years in the future when it was a hiking trail maintained by the park service.

The wolves were not around in the morning. They must have gone back to whatever shelter they called home. He took some of the entrails from one bear and scattered it down the grade just in case the wolves came back during the day. He blocked the entrance to the cave with boulders and set off for the pine tree landing area.

He cautiously pushed the pine tree he was using as his door out ahead of him into the early morning light that was beginning to turn the sky a dark grey.

He purposely left the tree blocking the path on the right. He wanted to prevent having wolves approach him from both sides in case they were still about and hunting him.

He proceeded out along the trail to his right. It went upward at roughly a thirty-degree angle.

He was carrying a ten foot long, three-foot-wide piece of the bear hide. He had now used up about half of the hide of one bear. He had another piece of hide that was about six foot long and three feet wide that he was making into a poncho for himself.

In the grey light of the early morning, he found the tracks he had made the day before and followed them downward toward his landing area.

He was within sight of the pine when he saw the pack of wolves traveling toward him at a slow walk.

He immediately picked up his pace. He decided that he would use the well of the tree as his point of defense. He could fight the wolves as they tried to get to him, or he could climb the tree to escape from them.

He saw the tracks that the wolves had made around the well of the tree. It was clear they had back tracked him the day before.

A quick glance over his shoulder let him know that he had a few moments before the pack would arrive.

He filled in the hole in the snow that he had made on his landing the day before. This effectively sealed an easy path in for the wolves.

Then after another quick look to locate the wolf pack he slid down into the well.

He immediately climbed up into the tree and secured the pieces of bear hide and then climbed high enough in the pine to see out of the well.

He almost fell when he looked out to the edge of the well into the dark black eyes of a huge dire wolf. He held tightly to the trunk of the pine as he recovered.

He realized that protecting Hanna and Eva from this pack was going to be a challenge.

He located his landing spot. Then he tried to estimate the weight of Hanna and Eva and estimated where they would land.

He threw a piece of the pine branch on the side of the snow to mark the location each would land.

He then climbed down to the base of the tree and went over to each marker and dug a tunnel outward from the tree trunk to the point where he thought each would land.

He cleared an area by the edge of the snow bowl where he could make a fire. He gathered the dead wood that was available and stacked it within reach of the fire area.

He had landed around the noon hour. He hoped the re-insertion would happen as close to that time as possible.

He climbed to the top of the pine. He was carrying the makings of his poncho with him to keep him occupied while he waited.

He reached the limb that allowed him to see easily across the top of the snow surface. The wolves were all sitting around the edge of the circle looking directly at him.

Adam looked back at each and counted thirty-three around the circle.

It was not looking good for Hanna and Eva.

Suddenly Adam felt electricity in the air. The wolves must have sensed it as well because they jumped up and began to whine or howl.

Adam looked upward about where thought the reinsertion would occur.

Suddenly Hanna came flying feet first from some thirty feet in the air. She hit the location Adam had estimated.

Adam slid rapidly down the tree and rushed over to the tunnel he had dug.

He immediately pulled down on Hanna's legs and got her into the well.

Adam turned to stare into the eyes of one of the dire wolves that had come down the hole. In one swift motion Adam grabbed his spear and drove it into the wolves chest.

The ease with which the blade cut through hide and bone reinforced the sharpness of the blade. A second wolf met the same fate.

Adam left both wolves in the hole to keep other wolves from getting through.

Hanna was still out.

Adam placed her on top of the hide and covered her.

He then climbed back up the tree to await Eva.

He spent the time scraping the fat from bear hide. He figured a poncho like covering would provide the needed protection from the cold until something better could be made.

He had formed a scraper by chipping an edge onto a flat rock and was now perfecting his use of his new tool.

His seat at the top of the pine allowed him to keep an eye on the surrounding territory. He gathered the fat he was scraping off. He would use it as fuel and later if there was any left, he planned to use it to distract the wolves if they were aggressive.

The afternoon passed slowly. About half of the wolf pack left but about twenty were still positioned around the well of the pine tree.

Adam finished scrapping the fat off the poncho and tried it on.

This time it was the reaction of the wolves that alerted Adam of Eva's impending arrival.

He concentrated on watching where she would land.

Eva came out headfirst. She must have been lighter than Adam had estimated as she landed a good two to three feet short of where he had dug the tunnel.

Adam rushed down; went into the tunnel he had excavated began to madly dig through the snow to where he hoped Eva would be.

He was digging so frantically that he put a scratch on her face.

He pulled her into the tunnel he had dug and caved in the snow so the wolves could not follow.

Eva was not breathing. Adam administered mouth to mouth and pumped her heart. He was rewarded a few moments later with Eva taking a deep breath on her own. He was surprised that she was still not awake.

He carried Eva over to where Hanna slept peacefully beneath the bearskin hide. He place Eva next to Hanna's left and covered them both.

He climbed the tree to get one last look at the area surrounding the well. He would need to figure out how to get the two back up to the cave.

The wolves were gone. It was time to make his move.

4 Re-Acquaintance

*T*he stars in the sky were stunningly beautiful. He remembered this same feeling the last time he had been at Yellow Stone as a scout.

The wolves had departed the area.

The moon was almost at its fullest and was now almost halfway across the sky.

Adam made the decision that it was time to get back to the safety of the cave.

He hastily skinned the two dead wolves and pulled their bodies up out of the tree well to the top of the snow. He dragged them out of the way and climbed down and carried Hanna and Eva up to the top. He then gathered the hide, spear, and poncho.

He tied the hide around the two women and began the long uphill pull to the cave.

He was pulling the two downhill feeling great about the successful uphill pull when a low throaty growl stopped him in his tracks.

Adam stopped pulling and raised his spear at the charging two wolves.

His spear found the chest of the wolf to his right. The wolf to his left leaped for his throat. Adam jammed his forearm hard as he could into the wolf's mouth. With his right hand he thrust his knife into the wolf's chest and pushed up and back.

The knife went in and cut back as if it was going through soft butter. None the less he heard the bone in his left arm crack as the light went out of the wolf's eyes.

Adam hurriedly pulled Hanna and Eva into the cave and pulled the dead pine tree to block the entrance.

He checked his arm and bound the punctures from the wolf's teeth.

His arm hurt!

He felt along the bone and concluded that it was probably cracked but not fully broken.

He heated up the soup with some hot stones and then used it to wash out the wound. He followed the washing by rubbing some of the bear fat over the wound.

After making sure Hanna and Eva were warm and appeared comfortable, he took one of their hands and held one in each of his and went to sleep.

He wanted to wake up when they did.

The morning light awoke him. Hanna and Eva were still asleep.

He concluded they would have all been dead, buried in the snow and eaten by the wolves if he had come through in the same sleeping condition that they had.

He wished he could send back a message to Emma.

There was one red coal left in the ash of the fire. Soon a fire was crackling, and bear meat was frying.

The two women were still out.

He heated the soup by putting in red hot stones.

He was beginning to understand the reason why Yellow Stone was the only acceptable re-insertion point, the snow, the cave, and his previous experience as an Eagle Scout.

The future knew who he was. It was a realization that sent a shiver down his back.

Finally, Hanna, the one with brown hair, brown eyes, the lithe one, stirred awake.

He had studiously been carving what he hoped would be a cup or bowl. He put in some stew and took it to her.

"You look like a cave man," were the first words from her lips.

He had taken the time to make a simple front and back flap covering him from the waist to mid-thigh.

He asked her if she was hungry as he handed her the soup. There were strips of meat sizzling on the fire behind him.

"Not bad. What is it and where am I," Hanna asked next after sipping on the stew?

"And where are my clothes, dammit," she exclaimed when she realized she was totally nude.

"Why don't any of us have any clothes," she said looking accusingly at Adam as she pulled a corner of the bear skin over her chest.

If you recall the last time, we were holding hands as our plane crashed. When Eva comes around, I will tell you a story you will find hard to believe. You will have no choice but to do so because of where you find yourself at this moment.

Just then, Eva, blond, blue eyes and the most endowed stirred awake.

He refilled the bowl and carried it to her.

"You're the guy from the plane. Where are we? Why are you almost naked?" she asked as she took the cup of soup.

I will fill you in on what has happened, Adam replied as he retreated across the room to sit on a comfortable rock.

"Begin with the reason we have no clothes," Hannah interjected and looked at Adam in an accusing manner.

"Let me begin back on the airplane. If you want some more soup, share the cup, and help yourself," He said and then proceeded to tell the story of how they got to the cave.

Eva at first did not believe the story. She asked Adam to give back her clothes.

Hanna stood up and walked over to the pine blocking the entrance to the cave.

"Forget your modesty and get over here and see what is in front of our cave," she said in a hushed tone.

Eva walked over to the cave entrance and looked to where Hanna was pointing.

Two dead wolves were laying in a deep red circle in the snow.

"Tell us what happened," Hanna said looking at Adam with new appreciation.

Adam recounted his arrival. He pointed to the hide and shared that two bears were awaiting in the back of the cave to be processed into food.

He then explained each of their arrivals.

Hannah decided to accept being naked.

Eva was not as comfortable and put on the poncho Adam had made.

They walked to the back of the cave and examined the dead bears.

He remained seated in the front of the cave. He wanted to give the two time to absorb the situation without his presence.

When the two returned to the front of the cave, Adam asked if either of the two knew how to sew.

"I have a feeling we all do. Every time I think about what we need, ideas sprout in my mind. I think we are loaded with survival and other key information." Eva responded.

Hannah replied that given Adam's story and what he heard, she thought they all probably knew how to sew. She went on to claim that the wolf hides and bear skin made her want to go hunt for some rabbits and foxes so she could have the proper materials for her new wardrobe.

Eva shared that she knew things about starting fires and cooking over a fire that she had never experienced in her life.

She finally accepted that the story Adam had shared was in fact true.

"I think we are loaded with survival and other key information." Eva responded.

He was surprised at how well the two had responded after their initial mistrust of his story. It was clear to them they were in a place and it appeared a time that was impossible to be unless his story were true, or they had died and gone to an alternate plane of existence.

The dire wolves outside their cave had also added a very convincing punctuation to his story.

Hannah took the lead in organizing their activities.

She asked what resources the three of them had.

Adam presented each of them their knives and explained how he had found them in the lab and later learned that they had been ordered by Emma, the leader of the Extraction and Re-insertion program, to be sent back with them. He had brought them through on his reinsertion.

He showed them his spearhead and the two that still needed to be mounted.

They went out for the first time on the following day to find three strong Oak or Maple branches to make into spear handles.

They used the sap from some pine trees and strips of hide to mount their spear heads.

Adam commented on the fact that they seemed to get along well.

Eva jokingly replied she had given up when she realized she was stuck with Hannah and him.

He pointed out that the purpose of being sent back was for them to procreate and enrich the human genome.

Emma in the future is looking for the impact the two of you have on the DNA of her time. She intends for you to be fruitful and multiply.

He then, with a slow western drawl, said he would be pleased to help them out.

He went on in a more serious tone and made the point that Emma was trying to get them reinserted into Europe but reinsertion connections for that location would not stabilize.

Somebody in the future, beyond Emma's time, knew something about the conditions we would face or perhaps failures in sending people back to other places. Or perhaps they knew of my intimate knowledge of this region.

History has no mention of a civilization in North America.

I think we need to make our way to Europe or North Africa. The folks sending us here wanted to put us there.

"I'm all for Europe," Hannah spoke up.

Eva agreed with Europe but asked which direction they should travel to get there.

Hannah suggested they travel northwest. She recalled that it was during this period that North America and Asia were connected by ice.

The three agreed and began their preparation for the trip.

Once the cave was secure as their home base, they began to hunt the surrounding territory.

They hunted together. All of them became skilled hunters.

The dire wolves were slow to learn that the three together presented a deadly force. Dire wolf hides represented more than half of the hide inventory the three accumulated.

Hannah had insisted they try the wolf meat to see if it was worth drying and keeping.

All three agreed that they did not care for its taste.

The bear, elk, rabbit, and ground hog meat provided more than their needs.

The salt in the cave allowed them to salt and dry the meat. It was immediately obvious they would be traveling and utilizing their dried meats as the primary source of sustenance.

They made sausage and used the cleaned entrails as the sausage skins.

They stretched and cleaned the hides of the bears, the elk, rabbits, groundhog, and wolves.

They put the cleaned skulls in the corner of the cave.

Adam knew the skulls would be there in his time. It would be he who would pack them in salt to preserve them through time. He knew he would also carve the message into the brain cavity of one of the skulls. As an Eagle Scout he would wonder who had written the message and what it meant.

They constantly discussed what they should do.

The rest of winter was spent preparing for the trip west to Europe.

The bear skin became the primary sleeping bed for the three of them.

They made Rabbit fur lined boots, gloves, and headdress.

The Elk provided leather for the soles of the boots and for tough outer jackets.

Adam planned ahead and carved the Elk leg bones into personally fitted snow glasses.

The time flew.

The three became a homogenous team.

They liked each other and enjoyed a constant banter.

Adam shared that he was with two of the most beautiful, adaptive, strong women he had ever dreamt he would be so privileged to be with.

Both Hannah and Eva came over to him and gave him a kiss.

Together they practiced Tae Kwon Do. Eva made the point that this ability would come in handy if they ran into other humans.

They held a ceremony each time Hannah rose up to a new belt level.

She and Adam were both black belts and soon they had Hannah's skill at their level.

Adam led Eva and Hannah to the young Elm trees he had located. Together they selected several of the trees that were the right size to make the bows and cut them and carried them to a warm water spring. There they put the put the wood into the water to soak.

Using the horn from the elk, the gut from the bear and the sap from the pine Adam was able to create a compound bow for each of them.

The three returned to the area where they had landed and selected cedar pine limbs to make the arrows.

The feathers of several geese and ducks provide the arrow guide feathering.

The three of them practiced chipping various stones until they had enough arrow heads.

The three of them practiced shooting until they were able to hit a moving target at about one hundred feet.

Eva demonstrated her superiority with the bow when one day she shot at and hit a running squirrel at over one hundred feet.

Adam put the squirrel into their stew for their evening meal.

After some discussion they decided March one on their calendar would be their departure date.

This would mean leaving the Yellow Stone in winter, but it would give them more time for crossing the Bearing Straight.

They would need to make very good time to make the crossing before the onset of winter. Even after crossing they would need go south and find a place on the Asian side where they could weather the winter.

The three discussed how best to carry their supplies on their upcoming trip.

They agreed that a sled to carry their food and shelter would be needed. Together they designed and built a long sled similar to the ones pulled by dog teams.

They added a unique feature not found on most sleds. They added two axels. The wheels were made of wooden slabs covered with leather. The wheel bearings were grease covered leather.

The three of them would be the power for the sled.

The sled was made wide enough so the load would be spread out for stability. A bed was made across the top.

The goal was to continue to travel throughout the night when there was enough light. They would take turns sleeping while the other two pulled the sled.

Adam made the point that they needed to make twenty miles a day if they wanted to get across ahead of the coming winter storms.

Hannah agreed and added that it was crucial they go far enough south to escape the extreme winter weather.

Adam brought the bear skull out into their living area and explained that he was going to carve a message to Emma, into the inside of the skull.

He already knew the message, so he guided the discussion until they agreed to the simple message: EM AEH Alive → EU

Hannah laughed and asked if they had agreed to the same message Adam had seen as Boy Scout in his time.

He recalled the shiver he had experience as an Eagle Scout when he had held the skull and read the message.

Adam carried the skull to the back of the cave and packed both skulls in the salt.

He knew this would last into his future time when he and his Dad would both spent the evening around the campfire talking about who and when had carved the cryptic message into the skull.

The next morning the three carefully loaded the sled.

They did a thorough cleaning of the cave and carefully sealed it.

Adam let Hannah and Eva know that the cave would be reopened in their time by two Forest Rangers who were clearing brush along the trail.

It would then become a tourist attraction.

Using his experience in riding the many trails and studying them for his Eagle Project, Adam led the way west along the Snake River.

They would follow it and later the Columbia. They would turn and go north and follow the long valley between the Rockies toward the middle of Alaska where they would go northwest until they hit the Bering Strait.

Then it was west in a long journey to Europe and a longer journey through time.

Out of the Garden of Eden to the world beyond.

5 *The Samuels*

arshal and his friend Sam each held a solid one inch oak stick about three feet long in their hands. The morning wind blew unobstructed across the open corn field. The bent cornstalks caught the blowing snow and formed snow tents where rabbits would take refuge from the cold.

The winter had been a constant succession of snowstorms. The snow was at least a foot deep with the occasional three-foot-high snow drift. They had found fresh rabbit tracks and were tracking them out into the field. They were carefully stepping over the dry bent corn stalks as they silently approached the stalk hiding their intended victim.

They looked at each other and in unison jumped over the last row and let their simple weapons swing in toward their target.

The rabbit leaped and dashed out to the right.

"He's mine," Marshall said as he put on a burst of speed and another swing at the rabbit.

"You're just too slow," Sam said as the rabbit turned sharply his way and he took a swing.

"He's mine," Marshall said as the rabbit made a fatal zig when he should have zagged.

The stick connected and the rabbit was on the way of becoming rabbit stew.

Marshal had listened to an old farmer claim to have hunted rabbits with only a stick. He had decided that he would try it. He felt that it was a fairer way to hunt. He was quite good at hunting with his four-ten, but he always felt that it was unfair to the game he was hunting.

A stick still gave him an advantage, but it was more of a challenge.

Life for Marshal became grounded by the surge of self-confidence that the power of a simple stick in his hands gave him.

Marshal thought back to the many times direct hands-on action solved his problems. He had a long successful career and constant proof of his ability for hands on action leading to success.

He was now moving into what he considered his last career, he was writing and once again he was walking his virtual corn field with a stick in his hand. He sought the mental stamina to, once again, swing that stick and make contact with the elusive rabbit.

This hands-on direct approach guided Marshal through his developing years. He served his time in the Vietnam War where he made sure the guns, he used only shot at someone firing first on him. He seldom pulled his trigger.

He returned from Vietnam and went on to become a US Navy nuclear reactor operator.

Then one Christmas, he volunteered to be on a new hydrofoil. The hydrofoil went on tour in Europe.

The hydrofoil crew flew on stainless steel wings in the water. It engaged in war games with the German high-speed gunboats in the North Sea.

The crew worked with the Danish Navy in exploring whether the sea mines could be tuned to counter the hydrofoil.

The Italian Navy gave he and the Hydrofoil crew a silver star for breaking new ground.

In Turkey, their counter parts threw them a party.

The tour of Europe was memorable and connected Marshal with the opinions of the world.

Marshal left the Navy and went on to get a master's degree in mechanical engineering.

In his second year at the University, he met the woman of his dreams.

For him it was love at first sight.

Nora never had a chance. Marshal had his stick in hand and ran just as fast as she.

When she zigged, he zagged?

He caught her and he made sure that he did everything possible to keep her.

They had three children: one girl and two boys.

Both He and Nora enjoyed careers and worked hard for many years.

Now almost forty years later, they were still in love.

They had raised their family and were now empty nesters.

The current work he did still provided the thrill it had on the day he started but his early passion to write had come to the surface.

It demanded equal time and screamed for his attention. He could not and did not want to deny it.

He made his decision.

His actions as always were direct to the point and swift.

"Nora, I am going to become a writer," Marshal announced to the love of his life.

"You can do whatever you want. What makes you think you can write and what will you write?" was her reply as she leaned over and gave him a peck on the cheek.

"I don't know that I can write or what I should write. I figure I'll give it a try. The worst that can happen is I will bore some poor readers," Marshal replied with a tone of confidence he was not really feeling.

He slept on it. He was sure action would go a long way in increasing his confidence.

For the first time in his life, he wished there were someone to give him guidance.

Since that first rabbit in the corn field, action had been the solution. He knew it would be no different in this case. The only difference was it was a new rabbit and one that could zig and zag in ways new to him.

He slept on it.

The next day he took action.

A few days later Marshal shared his writing interest with his oldest son Matt.

He had read some of Matt's college day writing and knew Matt was a very good writer.

He had encouraged Matt to write. Matt was busy getting his Web Site Development business going.

"Well, develop a web site for me. I'm buying; not asking a favor," Marshall told him.

Marshal put in his order for a website.

It was a major decision for him but for his oldest it was just another web site.

Matt had been a perpetual student. He began his school career pursuing computer science. He then decided on communication as his focus. He had two undergraduate degrees and a master's degree in communications and was currently completing a degree in Application Code Programing.

Matt had gone full circle back to his computer science passion and going into web development.

Changing focus was no big deal to him.

Andrew the younger son was a little more direct and challenging.

And asked some very direct and penetrating questions.

"What are you going to write about?

What makes you think anyone is going to read what you write?

He had been an editor for his school newspaper. Writing to him meant having a topic of interest or controversy to redress with several hundred or a thousand organized words.

Reading to him was to read the traditional writers.

He told me I should go read Huxley, T.S. Elliot, Stephen King, Asimov, Tolstoy, Emerson, Twain and then decide if I could do as well.

I listened and I read. It provided great insight and it provided a great deal of learning. I recognized Andrew's feedback and questions as the same ones coming from his mind.

I had never been limited by my fear and though I doubted that I could write like the great "greats" I would write. What I recognized and learned was that the greats had many writing that had not been so great.

I knew fear would make me work harder, dig deeper and persevere until I succeeded

I preferred the saying, "Fools rush in where Angels fear to go."

I decided to celebrate the change in careers by taking a grand family vacation.

I scheduled the whole family into the Yellowstone Park Lodge.

I invited the family to watch Old Faithful from the porch of the hotel.

We drove up the Interstate in from the airport in Salt Lake City. The approached to the park was from the west on state route 191. It was just after lunch as we followed the signs indicating the way to Old Faithful.

We were all chatting and enjoying the ride, but all talk stopped in mid-sentence and we forgot what we were talking about as we took in the size of grandeur of the Old Faithful Inn.

It caught all of us by surprise.

The building was massive with an observation deck across the top that seemed to be a crown atop the steeply pitched cedar shingle roof that began on the second floor and went steeply up past multiple gables to support its heavenly crown adorned with an American flag bracketed by two additional flags on each side.

The building exuded a sense of shelter. Its massive size was a perfect match to the majesty of the snow-capped peaks surrounding it.

We immediately connected the comfort and beauty of the Inn as a bridge with the unpredictable, wild world around it.

Matt likened it to a sentinel guarding the valley and providing the visitor a way to observe the wild and the wonderful.

Marshal stopped to absorb the image of seven stories of beams supporting the steeply pitched shingled roof. The image of his three-pronged frog gig came immediately to mind as he scanned the seven stories of the three-pronged eight inch in diameter tree supports selected as the vertical support members. He noted that many of the gabled dormers were purely decorative.

Matt pointed to the massive fireplace with multiple hearths with the chimney extending to the roof. The Iron work clock seemed functional as Matt checked it against his Fit Bit.

Marshal walked across the lobby and checked the family in. He had reserved four rooms. One for Nora and him, one for Matt and Andrew and the other two for Serena and her kids.

Marshal had originally suggested dinner at a restaurant in Jackson Hole but realized that suggestion was impractical.

Andrew suggested they take a short jog and then have dinner in the lodge dining room.

There was immediate agreement.

The four asked the desk clerk for a recommendation of where to jog.

Andrew led the way as they followed the path that had been suggested. Marshal brought up the rear as they left the large crowd around the Old Faithful area and jogged up a long slow upward slope that leveled off at the top and narrowed along a steep ridge.

They took the right-hand fork that soon made a hair pin turn and descended on a narrow path back parallel to their outward jog. The path led to a cave that had recently been opened for tourists and they were once again back in a crowd of people with back packs and hiking boots.

They returned to the lodge and agreed to meet in the dining room after a quick shower.

Marshal took in the less massive but still impressive fireplace in the dining room. He selected a table that centered the family in front of the fireplace. He knew Nora would be taking pictures and having the waiter or waitress take pictures. The fireplace would be a perfect background.

Nora was in the lobby taking pictures, a few minutes later she followed him in and praised him for the table selection.

After forty years of marriage, Marshal was still madly in love and just smiled at the too familiar words.

Matt and Andrew came in chatting. Matt stopped so suddenly that Andrew bumped into him.

Andrew's sharp brotherly reaction and small push did not get the normal rise from Matt.

Matt came over to the table but seemed distracted by a young lady sitting by herself at a table to the side of the fireplace area.

Marshal asked Matt what was so distracting.

Matt's reply stopped the conversation at the table.

"I am looking at my future wife," was his quiet reply.

The comment triggered Marshal's memory of his similar comment when, as a young college student, he had first seen Nora.

He looked over at the profile of a young blonde lady with a lithe runner's body. She was by herself reading a book about two inches thick. This to him meant that she was by herself.

The waitress arrived with the menu. It seemed basic and Marshal ordered a hamburger, and sweet potato fries.

The Nora ordered a salad.

Matt and Andrew decided to share a pizza.

Marshal ordered a tea and once again glanced over to the young lady.

He was surprised when Matt got up and walked over to where she was sitting.

Andrew commented that he had never seen Matt act this way.

Marshal watched as Matt entered into a conversation.

When the dinner arrived, Marshal stood up and walked over, introduced himself and invited the two to join them at the family table.

Her name was Samantha. Her deep blue eyes seemed to penetrate into his.

He noted that the book was the collected works of Henry David Thoreau.

Marshal and Nora were in the lobby when Serena and her family arrived. He watched as they too stopped to take in the lobby of the Inn.

The twin granddaughters came over and got a hug.

After all the hugging was over, they checked in and went to their rooms.

They agreed to meet for a late breakfast

Marshal woke up before sunrise. This was unusual for him. He was a night person but for some reason he was awake, and Nora was sound asleep.

He got up and put on his running shorts and went out to put on his shoes and go for a quick morning jog.

He was surprised to see Samantha jog past him. He could see her ear plug pieces and knew she listened to music as she jogged. He finished tying his shoes and jumped up to catch up to her.

It was clear to Marshal that Samantha was in great shape. He was keeping pace but not closing the gap.

She was on the same trail the family had taken the afternoon before.

Marshal decided to push himself and catch up.

He was puffing like an old steam engine by the time they both reached the top of the trail.

Marshal pushed himself and made a dash to get in front of her so she would see him.

Just as he pulled up even and was about to pass her, it happened.

Marshal thought he had tripped and fallen off the cliff. It definitely felt as if he were falling. He looked down at himself and realized he was totally naked.

He figured he must have had a heart attack and died. Everything around him seemed to be black.

There to his right, looking like a sleeping goddess was Samantha. She too was totally naked.

He figured that Matt would not be very pleased to know that in dying Marshal was fantasying about her.

He reached out to see if the image was real and was shocked when his hand made contact with her arm.

She was real.

At least to Marshal's current situation she seemed real.

She appeared to be unconscious. He put his finger to her neck to check her pulse. He found a slow but steady one. Her eyelids were twitching as if she were experiencing REM sleep.

It seemed unusually cold. They were falling somewhere to some place.

How they would land was now becoming Marshal's concern.

He decided to pull Samantha to him. He folded her arms across her chest and held her back to his chest.

He would be in deep trouble if she came awake as he held her. Marshal imagined Samantha screaming and accusing him if she awakened.

This situation reminded Marshal of the time he tried to save a drowning sailor who fought to drown both of them in the process. Even after saving the sailor, he got cursed for trying to drown him.

Then Marshal saw the light. It was like looking out into daylight from a dark cave or the tunnel of the underground subway emerging to the surface.

He knew instinctively they were about to make their landing. He turned so he would land on his back. This would cushion the landing and would protect Samantha from being crushed by his landing on her.

He figured her for a little over one hundred pounds and now he knew she was about five foot, five inches and well proportioned.

He had seen and knew more than she ever intended him to know or see about her.

Just before hitting he slammed his hand on the flat surface, let out a loud yell and bam! The landing was not as bad as he had thought it would be. It did knock the breath out of him.

Momentarily the wind was knocked out of his lungs, but he did not pass out. He rolled Samantha off to his side and jump up in a fighting stance as three fully suited figures out of a science fiction movie stood before him.

Marshal heard someone make the point that there were two extractions.

The English was a little stilted but understandable.

He recognized the suits as decontamination suits.

One of the figures held an ugly gun like object.

The room went silent, and everything seemed to stand still. Marshal assumed his Tae Kwon Do fighting pose and almost burst out laughing as he pictured himself. He was a naked old man. At six foot two and one hundred sixty pounds he was the largest person in the room.

"Stop everything and explain the situation, where I am and when I am." Marshal said in a clear commanding voice.

A smooth, comforting female voice seemed to float into the room. Sir we intend no harm to you nor Samantha.

You are in the extraction receiving decontamination room. The three technicians need to provide medical assistance to Samantha.

The explanation made sense. It was clear he was an unexpected second person and the person talking knew Samantha's name but not his.

I am Emma, please let the technicians administer their shot so Samantha does not go into shock.

I have someone bringing some clothes and she will escort you to an interview room.

Marshal heard the technician call out Samantha's vitals and comment that they were weak but that she had suffered no broken bones.

Marshal took the offer of clothes and made it clear he was not going to let Samantha out of his sight until he was sure about the situation, they found themselves in.

He held her hand as she was placed on a gurney and pushed down the hall.

A hologram appeared in the room they entered. Marshal was able to recognize it as the monitoring and control center for Samantha.

Marshal watched as Samantha was lifted and placed on the bed. The mattress seem to form around her.

He looked at the one technician that remained in the room when the three suited ones left and asked about the bed and the mattress.

Marshal listened as the technician explained that everything entering and leaving Samantha's body was being handled by the mattress.

The technician went on to explain that the system would monitor her condition and optimize all the vital signals.

Another technician came in with what appeared to be a pale blue gown with edge strips.

Marshal accepted some help in getting it on and then was somewhat amazed as the material adjusted itself to his body It was a perfect fitting jump suit with two front pockets.

There was no place to sit so he paced slowly back and forth trying to make sense of where he was.

His situation was similar to many of the imagined plots he concocted for his writing. He was surprised that his imagination had so accurately depicted the events he was now experiencing.

His previously concocted scenarios provided a wealth of response options and made it easier for him to accept what would otherwise seem impossible.

Emma was intrigued by the old man extracted with Samantha.

His appearance explained the much higher energy surge required for this extraction.

Having someone show up fully awake was even more unexpected and unnerving. There was no protocol for this situation. Worse, there was no historic record of his disappearance from his time frame.

What would she do with this person? Should this person be forcibly put to sleep?

Her extraction team wanted to debrief him to find out details about the extraction experience.

Emma took a deep breath and then walked through the door and looked at the person standing looking steadily back at her. This person was not at all intimidated. He seemed to be in full control.

She had expected a confused, unsure individual.

At six two Marshal stood almost a foot above the attractive young woman with emerald, green eyes and pixy cut black hair.

She seemed to hesitate, so Marshal continued with a full introduction.

He suggested that he was in the future and that his extraction had been a mistake. He went on to make the statement that he, unlike other extractions, came in awake.

You are Emma, the voice I heard in the landing area. You are trying to figure out what to do with me.

He watched her face looking for any signs of surprise. He decided not to play poker for money with her.

Marshal stopped and declared that it was Emma's turn to talk.

Emma was impressed at how much Marshal had correctly guessed. She took an immediate liking to him. She complemented him on his guesses.

How far into the future are we Marshal inquired?

Emma's reply of five hundred years caused Marshal to let out a low whistle.

You are in almost the exact location of your extraction. This caused Marshal to think about his long fall.

Marshal looked over to Samantha and asked how long it would be before she would be awake.

Emma briefly explained that the extracted person was never awakened in this time period. They normally remained asleep and were reconditioned until they were re inserted into the distant past.

Marshal gave Emma a smile and asked what she was going to do with him.

Emma's response suggested that if he allowed them to do so they would take him through the same treatments they gave the other extractions. This would extend his life span by several hundred years.

Since they had never had someone come through awake, they were interested in his experience and account of the extraction.

They would also like to understand how he had managed to escape their very thorough analysis of the extraction time period.

Marshal immediately suggested they put some foam rubber to soften the landing area

Emma inquired about how he felt and if he would care for something to eat and led Marshal out of Samantha's room.

Marshal commented that breakfast if it were the right time would be great.

Later, seated comfortably in a large, padded chair that seemed to fit itself to him, Emma asked him to explain his comment about landing in the Extraction room.

Marshal explained the long continuous free fall, the appearance of the white light and the impact. He shared how he had controlled his landing and protected Samantha, otherwise bone would most likely have been broken.

Emma shared that they were not aware that it was a falling experience for the person being extracted. They observed the arrival as the body suddenly appearing on the floor in the middle of the receiving area.

The landing area and the extraction site are at the exact same elevation.

Marshal speculated that perhaps it was time he had fallen through. He then chuckled and commented that it was good she had not been some ten thousand years in the future.

Marshal suggested the creation of a well filled with some shock absorbent material. He suggested they match the exact elevation to the top of the soft surface otherwise the person being extracted might end up embedded in the material.

Emma looked at Marshal and asked him if he had a son named Matt and one named Andrew. She was not sure how to let Marshal know about the next two extractions.

Marshal's introduction of himself had caused her whole team to react in amazement. Something in the history timeline had gone wrong or had changed. It was too much of a coincidence that the next two extractions would be his two sons.

Marshal was caught off guard by the question, but he knew instantly who the next two extractions would be.

He looked steadily back at Emma and simply asked why these three?

Marshal remained absolutely still as he looked around the room.

He was glad he had tried catching up to Samantha.

The thought of Nora and the pain she would experience by the mysterious disappearance three of her family was very troubling to him.

His only consolation was that Serena was there to comfort her.

He repeated his question of why these three?

Emma explained that they studied every person to be extracted for many years before selecting and executing the extraction. She explained that Matt and Andrew and Samantha die in a car accident in Jackson Hole on the night after you and Samantha got extracted.

I was able to precisely place Samantha, Matt, and Andrew on the trail at the extraction location.

I got special permission to extract them prior to the accident in hopes of getting them here with no broken bones.

I know many details about you. You are an impressive individual but not on our extraction list. History shows you remain in your time and become a prolific writer.

Marshal looked at Emma and replied in that case he would relax because he indeed planned to fulfill his place in history.

He pointed out that if the three disappeared the accident would not occur. He asked how history handled the mystery of four people missing from Yellowstone.

Emma replied that the team could tell from historic records only three people went missing. A search was conducted. No bodies were found. After a few weeks, the issue became a cold case.

Nothing more related to this incident occurs until a few years later. Then a group will come back to this site and we will do one more extraction. It seems the woman who organized a commemorative ceremony for your son Andrew, will fall off the cliff at the time of the ceremony. We will be there to catch her.

Marshal thought about Andrew's singing ability and his online singing videos.

He asked about the third extraction and when it was schedule and learned that it was about a year out.

Marshal realized that this team had studied his family in detail.

Emma shared that the Samuels family went on to prosper and do well. You seemingly ran a successful publishing company and stories in your name continued to be published for many years. Either you have left behind a strong backlog or your wife found someone to ghost write for you.

Marshal contemplated his situation. He realized Emma had missed one potential explanation. He filed this realization away for later review and analysis.

He asked if Emma had ever sent back anyone to their extraction time?

She replied that doing so would have little impact on their current time frame. They were doing the reinsertions as far back as possible in hopes that time would provide the improvement in the human strain.

She quickly went on to explain that even in his case if they decided to try their current reinsertion accuracy would be plus or minus several hundred years.

Marshal asked why there was such interest in accelerating human development.

Emma deflected his question and let him know that she would act on his suggestion on the preparation for the next extraction.

She told him she needed to get this work scheduled to get done as fast as possible. Meanwhile she asked him to begin his rehabilitation.

Emma promised to send material for him to study. Then we will spend some more time together to figure out what to do with you.

Let me escort you to the living quarters that have been arranged for you. It is actually the living quarters of one of the associates in this facility. I think in your time you would call it an apartment.

She and her team wanted to have a window of time in which to continue to study Marshal's situation.

Marshal asked to be present at the extraction of his two sons. He also requested to come back and check on Samantha.

Emma replied that she would verify his participation in the extraction and that her team wanted to spend some time debriefing him in the next day or so.

Marshal quietly followed Emma. He hoped there would be a computer or some other communications connection that he could get on. He hoped he would be able to figure out how to interface with the technology of this time period.

6 Marshal

Emma was lost in thought and in listening to her team discussion as she walked down the hallway with the mystery person from the past. Her team members were all talking and postulating ideas of how this could have happened.

For some reason she felt Marshal represented answers to many questions. His ability to grasp the situation, analyze it and then participate in meaningful discussion was beyond what she had expected.

The human race needed a break.

It was being squeezed by the random decay of the DNA strand and at this very moment superior alien forces were challenging it. Her primary and original team was focused on improving the DNA strand and resilience.

However, she had been called to action and was now the leader of another team currently focused on dealing with an Alien threat

This second team was losing ground rapidly.

She wondered whether Marshal could provide any help in that field.

Emma was surprised at Marshal's confidence and a seeming ability to rapidly adjust.

She had been called to lead the communication with this alien team.

She assigned one of her team members to take Marshal to his apartment and get him settled.

Marshal shook hands with the person introduced as Leslie. It was clear to him that Emma was handing over the job of getting him settled to Leslie.

Emma made the point that he should ask for whatever he wanted or needed, and Leslie would do her best to provide it.

Marshal followed Leslie as Emma turned and walked back the way that they had come. He called to her and said he hoped to see her later that day.

Marshal followed Leslie into the apartment.

He immediately realized that he did not recognize anything but the pictures and these seemed to be a part of the wall.

What he took to be a potential easy chair looked more to him like a cream puff. It was sitting at the end of a potential cream puff couch. A large black glass, four foot by four foot, sixteen-inch-high object that could pass for a coffee table was in the center of the room and about a foot away from the chair and couch.

Marshal asked Leslie to explain the various objects in the room and if there was any way for him to get himself familiar with the major events that had transpired in the last few hundred years and a quick understanding of current day culture.

Leslie pointed to the black coffee table and said that it was the latest information cube available.

The cube came on as Leslie explained that she had received her implant connection to the worldwide when she was a kid.

She went on to explain that she had learned to isolate herself or to engage at any time from any place.

Marshal asked whether she was able to send and receive any time she wanted.

Leslie reassured him that it was as easy as thinking about going fishing while talking to someone about their problems. Leslie clarified that a person could send what they saw and heard much like a camera but that they could not send their thoughts. What a person speaks can be heard by those connected.

Marshal thought back on his discussions with Emma and realized that the long pauses she sometimes took were probably when she was listening to the team she kept talking about.

Marshal looked at the cube and wondered how he was going to get it to work for him. He had no chip implants. He stood and watched the information and visuals that Leslie had activated. Marshal thought of it as a three-dimensional holographic television.

Marshal walked around the cube impressed by the detail and life like appearance of the scene before him.

He immediately like it and asked if there was a way for him to use it.

Leslie stopped talking for a minute and seemed to stare at Marshal.

He immediately knew she was listening to someone via her world-wide connection.

Leslie blinked once and replied that she had just requested that the unit remain on until she ordered it to go off.

Marshal went through a series of questions.

How do I get something to eat?

How do I pay for what I order?

Do people still eat meat?

Can I order a hamburger and French fries?

How do I get a good book to read?

How do I open and close the door?

Leslie listened to each question and replied that everything could be done via the communication cube.

People ate vegetable-based hamburger, but the meat of animals had not been use for several hundred years. Books were read mentally online or had them read to them.

The door stumped her and after the blank stare she replied that unfortunately he was locked in until he could have his DNA put into the system.

Marshal asked Leslie to guide him through ordering a Chinese dinner and show him how to take a shower. He said he was ready to relax.

He was ready to get Leslie out of the room. He was sure he was being watched and listened to. Anything he did in the apartment would be documented.

"Oh, let me take you through the hygiene practices of today. No one has taken a water shower for more than two hundred years. Let me show you how a revitalizer works, Leslie replied. "You step in nude, tune it to revitalize and wait for the green light to come on. When it does, you press the moisturize button and you will feel tingly all over. That's it,"

"Let me quickly show you the other personal hygiene matters," Leslie said, and she went on to explain the use of the restroom. Everything was significantly different.

Marshal was glad he had asked about a shower. He would never have figured out how to use anything if Leslie had not demonstrated how to do it.

He thanked Leslie for her detailed explanations and the how-to demonstrations. He went to the cube and placed his order.

I will get something to eat and then wait for Emma to come back this evening," Marshal said with a tone indicating he was through asking for more understanding.

Leslie left and Marshal went carefully around the room to see if he could recognize any monitoring devices. He was not sure he could recognize one if he were looking directly at one.

The room was very simply decorated and did not appear to have been prepared for him. It truly seemed to be a plain room used by one of the personnel.

He then went about learning to use the cube. He wondered about the security the cube might have.

In fact, it seemed to have none.

He tried looking himself up. No luck.

He tried Emma, extraction technology; and got an immediate hit. He was just getting into learning about this when there was a call from the door.

Marshal stood up and just said, "Yes, what is it?"

I am delivering food, may I come in?

"Sure, please do so."

As the delivery boy brought in the food, an idea came to Marshal.

If a delivery boy could walk in through his door, could he walk out with him?

He had walked in with Leslie.

"Could you wait a moment," he asked the young man.

Marshal went to his cube and ordered a pizza for a six PM delivery. If his idea worked, he needed a way back in.

He then escorted the Chinese food delivery boy out. He walked parallel to him and together they walked through the door. He was smart enough to take the sack of Chinese food with him.

"How do you get back to your place of work?" Marshal asked.

The young man looked at him as if he were deranged, "I just get on the mover and return the way I came."

"Great, can I come along," Marshal said nonchalantly.

Marshal followed the young man and was amazed as they traveled along what essentially was a moving sidewalk. There were three narrow lanes. The initial one was slow moving. The middle one moved at a moderate rate and the outer one moved at a brisk pace. It traveled the same trail down the mountain to the lodge in Yellowstone he had jogged prior to his extraction.

Marshal followed the young man as he went onto the high-speed lane and then came back down as they approached the lodge.

There they both got off.

When he asked about the destination of the additional people movers, he was given a strange look by the food deliverer, but he was told that it went to Jackson Hole and from there bigger enclosed people movers connected to various cities in the country.

Marshal took note that the area around the lodge had been returned to a more natural state and seemed wilder.

The lodge had been preserved in all of its grandeur.

He was immediately in a familiar place. The massive fireplace looked just the same as the first time he had seen it. Marshal wondered if any of the wood in the lobby was the original wood from his time. He doubted it would be.

The three large information cubes in the lobby were immediately obvious to him. He was relieved to see that they were all in the activated state.

He approached the cube no one was using. It was larger than the one in his room.

He went in search of his DNA. After several tries, he came to the conclusion there was no way to get it. He was from too far in the past and his DNA was not on record.

He decided to learn about the current situation in the world.

Every venue was broadcasting the fact that four massive alien star ships were in their solar system.

Marshal now knew that Emma's reference to outside threats really meant Alien invasion.

Contact had been made with another race whose purpose of coming to Earth was colonization. This race had prospected the Earth millions of years earlier. At the time of their scouting, no intelligent live was encountered.

The aliens were surprised that intelligence had risen so quickly. They had committed a large portion of their civilization to this colonization venture.

They offered to share the Earth with the Earthlings. But the Earthlings rejected such a notion and now a full-scale global war was going on and Earth was losing.

Marshal sat back letting it all sink in.

Being transported to the future was one shock.

Knowing his sons would be pulled into the future was another shock.

Alien invasion was the final straw.

About now he was really identifying with the story of Rip Van Winkle.

He continued to scan the news and information trying to understand the battle plan and strategy being used to fight against the aliens.

It appeared the Earth was only taking a defensive versus offensive approach.

Marshal wondered why?

He wondered if the time transport system could be used to insert fighters into the alien ships.

How could they overcome this invasion?

He found himself immersed in the confrontation.

The afternoon melted away as he followed one thread of investigation and learning after another.

He almost missed the Pizza delivery boy leaving the lodge. He hurried after him and caught up at the people mover.

At the apartment he introduced himself and walked in with the Pizza deliverer.

Marshal felt good about his ability to get out and back into his apartment. He chuckled to himself as he thought about needing to manage the calorie allocation limits as he made use of the food delivery system.

He had found a means of gaining some independence. This alone gave him great confidence.

He would need to learn more. His five hour use of the info cube in the hotel had earned him many nasty looks, from what he took as tourists and hotel guests, but it had proved invaluable.

Marshal was thinking about his upcoming dinner with Emma when he heard her asking permission to come in.

He had made it back just in time.

Emma came in through the door and smelled the aroma of a mushroom, cheese pizza. She said she was ready for a piece.

She took in a rejuvenated Marshal.

"He must have used the rejuvenator after his day of sleep," Emma thought to herself.

"Well, I have good news. The team wants to get you acclimated to the current time and to debrief you. We are very interested in your travel here. We would also like to get your perspective on some other matters."

"You mean you want my opinion about your losing battle against the alien invasion," Marshal replied.

He watched as Emma stopped talking and closed her eyes.

It was clear to him that she was trying to overcome the mental noise of her team.

"Have a seat, isolate yourself from your team and then the two of us can talk," Marshal continued.

"I'm not sure what you are talking about," Emma replied as she isolated herself from her team and wondered how Marshal could possibly have known.

"Tell me you are isolated, or you don't get a piece of your favorite pizza."

She had slipped for only a moment but in that instance, Marshal gained enough self-confidence to plunge assertively forward.

He was a mean card player, and he knew he had to play his hand while he had the advantage.

"I have spent the afternoon learning about your extraction and insertion program. I know you are always online, linked through to the world-wide. This probably means your extraction team has been with us from the beginning. Are they still with you?" Marshal asked.

"No, I have isolated myself from them," Emma replied. "How did you learn about the connection?"

"I learned it from Leslie. She was explaining to me how I could read by using the world-wide connection. This led me to learn about the ability for multiple people to stay connected." Marshal replied.

"I have learned about the battle going on with the Aliens. Earth is losing this confrontation. If you were in a battle with the people of my time you would already have lost. There is too much available information on your cube and if I can get to it so can the Aliens.

Your defensive strategy is a sure loser. If you want to win you will have to take the battle to the Aliens instead of waiting for them to attack. Your loses will be higher but so will theirs and your only advantage that I can see is you out number them ten to one.

I want to help," Marshal ended as he ran out of breath.

He handed Emma a piece of pizza.

Emma looked at Marshal in amazement.

The team had monitored the information cube and knew of no activity for the entire day and afternoon.

They had assumed Marshal had fallen asleep.

How had he gotten all the information?

He somehow knew what cheese and that she liked extra mushroom with her favorite pizza.

Marshal asked how the work for the next extraction was coming.

Emma replied that the work had been completed. The soft-landing pad had been counter sunk into the floor.

She informed him that she had arranged for him to be present for the extraction.

How did you get all the information you have obtained?" Emma asked in total confusion.

Finally, Emma asked how he had learned so much without using the information cube.

Marshal promised to tell her but that they should concentrate on the pizza before it got cold.

He followed with a question about her re-insertion logic and the reasoning behind it.

He wanted to change the focus from him to the work Emma was leading.

The deflection worked.

Marshall sat back and listened intently to Emma's explanation of the project. He was pleased to have someone feeding him information. Getting it, himself had been a constant onslaught on his limited capability.

The five-hundred-year time gap made so many things seem unbelievable.

Marshal listened to Emma as her explanation flowed out in what he was sure was a practiced speech.

"More and more mistakes are showing up in the human DNA strand. I have been working for more than one hundred years on the concept of sending women back twenty-five or thirty thousand years. The goal is to seed the past with healthy future DNA and accelerated the development of the human species.

This finally became a reality when worm holes could be generated in time. These time worm holes are locked to one extraction location by situating the extraction system at the exact point an available person will be at a specific time. This allows us to extract their time into our time. So, the extraction points are worm holes to the future. The worm holes to the distant past work in a similar fashion but we have less control as to placing the person and success will only be verified by a change in the DNA.

So far there are no documented successes.

"You are sending people into the past. Perhaps their landing is as bad or worse that what I experienced. If that is the case, your reinsertion may be killing those you are sending back," Marshal suggested.

Emma put her pizza down. She admitted that she and her team had come to the same conclusion as they examined the landing pad they had installed.

"We have tried six times. But we must send them back that far to be of any use. What are we going to do now?" Emma said dejectedly.

"You have to come up with a better re-insertion technique," Marshal replied.

"You need to figure out how to ensure your subjects are dumped into a lake feet first or devise some other means of reinserting. Also, I think the fall rate stabilizes. At first, I thought I was picking up speed, but the increase seemed to slow. Perhaps there is an upper speed limit," Marshal conjectured.

Several re-injection ideas come to mind.

"You know, I am bushed. I am not sure how long I have been without sleep. I do know I am very tired. I am not sure how I get a bed so I can sleep," Marshal said realizing he had not asked Leslie how to get a bed.

He was sure he would ask for a bed in the room, and one would appear.

Emma asked for a bed and the couch changed shape.

She realized that Marshal had directed the discussion. He seemed to purposely steer it away from the current battle going on with the Aliens.

7 Caligrians, The Fold, the Fall

The fall as Maltar and as everyone in the Space Corp called the transfer was longer this time. The team was seated in the main control room. They were strapped into cushioned, and spring supported chairs.

The team had successfully experienced dozens of shorter falls.

Maltar's tight knit team operated smoothly. He had driven them to excel and had constantly worked the politics during mission selection time. His team had become the lead team because he always promised and delivered success.

He was driven to be the first to find a new home for his people.

His team knew and admired his drive and supported him with a loyalty all observers knew was absolute.

Maltar was not only the leader but the tallest and strongest on the team. The fine, thin covering of hair on his skin was black. The black swept black hair on his head, though similar to everyone's hair made him a commanding, good looking figure. Early in his career he had been known as a lady's man.

Since taking command of the exploration team, he had been too busy.

The team was a mix of blacks, browns, and tans. The other distinction was each of the three variations had distinct eye color. Maltar's almost pure black eyes gave him an ominous look. The browns had brown eyes. The tans sported yellow eyes.

The mix of these features was becoming more prominent as the barriers between the races disappeared.

Maltar was a black, a member of the ruling class. This at least was the historic background of the blacks. Even after thousands of cycles, this historic distinction was still present.

He was the son of a famous early planetary leader and enjoyed the benefit of this connection. This connection opened the top military colleges to him. He enlisted in the space core and his skill and drive took him up through the ranks.

Though proud of his family's long and prominent history as leaders of his planet, Maltar had used his own skills and capabilities to get to where he was in the Space Core.

His bravery and willingness to take risk earned him recognition and the assignment to be the leader of the first time-fold space explorer team.

He had handpicked his team based on their skill. He never considered their gender or color, only their capability, desire to win and their fit with the other team members.

His team had three black, three tan and only one brown.

Maltar discovered browns excelled in the social and religious endeavors but only a few were interested in the hard technical sciences associated with the exploration of space.

Maltar and his generation were the first of the population to benefit from the greatly increased life expectancy. He was now three hundred and twenty cycles old and had reached what was now considered mid-life. The generation before him had perished in what had then been the normal time of one hundred twenty cycles.

The world population had bulged with the age increase but then settled out at a new level based on the extended life. It turned out life was extended but regeneration remained something done early in the life cycle.

Maltar had never mated and had no offspring. He was uncle to six and great uncle to fourteen.

All three distinct variations of Caligrians, the blacks, the browns and the tans enjoyed the same long-life span.

Equality was the pride of the current Caligrian Society. The social battles between the three groups continued in a refined quiet political back-room way. Mixed mating was now common. It was obvious that in some distant future, the tans would be the dominant color.

This time they were going through the fold for the exploration of an extremely distant solar system. The team was prepared for the longer fall but they had no clue as to its length.

The Caligrian scientists had developed a way to fold space and to send objects across the fold. The effect of falling seemed to be proportional to the distance being crossed.

In their previous falls they had determined there was a maximum rate to the fall and the landing impact was proportional to the time of fall.

Over the dozen falls the control room, equipment and the clothing used by the team used were all improved.

The scientist estimated fifteen to twenty hours for their current fall. No chances were taken. The crew sat in their spring and air cushioned chairs the entire twenty hours.

Maltar turned down the brightness of the projection. He and six other explorers let out a cheer as the system enhanced the three-dimensional image in the center viewing area.

They had emerged in toward the center of the planetary system. As postulated, several smaller planets orbited close in near the star. There were giant planets farther out in this same system. These larger planets had been predicted based on the wobble of the central star.

The inner ones were new discoveries and the ones of interest to the team.

One of the crew members brought out a bottle of Nasadi and seven glasses.

"To our success at finding a suitable planet for our people," she toasted after everyone picked up their glass.

"To our success," Maltar reiterated.

He looked around at his team as he set his glass down.

He pointed to the two planets that he wanted to get surveyed before their thirty cycles of exploration time were up.

Maltar ordered launch of their scanning systems.

He then simply said, Let's roll.

Maltar pointed to the projection of the third planet. He zoomed the scanners in and ordered the ship to get in as close as possible to the planet.

Maltar studied the projection of the planet in the viewing area. He was now able to zoom in and study the surface in more detail. Shortly the ship would be in orbit and possibly descend to the surface. Samples of air, water and land would be collected for more detailed study.

The scanners showed the fourth planet to have a shallow covering of water in some deep canyons and a thin atmosphere. Indications of life were strong. To find life on two planets was an unexpected finding.

This was the first life to be found beyond their home planet. They would need to visit both planets.

The third planet captivated Maltar. He could not get over its abundance. It was bursting with life. Multiple excursions to the surface verified no intelligent life existed.

The one rule the Caligrian leadership held inviolate was any planet with intelligent life was to be off limits.

The third planets size was exactly that of the home planet.

Maltar concluded he and his team had discovered the planet that would allow his home world to escape its dying and expanding sun.

Maltar's biggest concern was the fact that the planet was teaming with animal life. What if some species developed intelligence prior to his peoples return?

He decided to ensure there would be no intelligence when he returned.

He deflected an asteroid so it would hit the planet.

His crew, though not in total agreement with the action, went along with him.

They watched as the asteroid struck the midsection of the planet. The impact threw up millions of tons of material. A dust cloud enveloped the planet.

Maltar was sure that this action would halt the evolution of the giant creatures abundant on the planet.

He felt little remorse. He felt justified in his action because he would save the lives of billions of his people.

He would ensure his intelligent species would prevail.

Maltar looked out at the system one more time before giving the command to activate the fold power transmitter.

When the navigator replied that they were at the fold location, Maltar simple said Fold.

The fall back was uneventful, and they returned only two days later then when they had left.

The return was historic. Maltar and his team became instant heroes. Their projections of the planet went viral. They were engulfed in celebration and technical discussions.

Maltar immediately acted to leverage the influence the discovery of habitable planetary system gave him.

The leaders of the dying Caligria solar system agreed to put Maltar in charge of the entire migration program. They promoted him to Sovereign Commander, a military term that at one time meant ultimate power.

Maltar humbly accept the promotion but he was thrilled to be given such control.

He sent out search vessels in all directions across the universe. He saw it as a time for the thirty billion Caligrians to leave their home planet and establish the Caligrian Empire.

With their new technology they would be able to maintain a common connection even when located on planets millions of light years apart.

Maltar recognized that even with the solid alignment to the migration, the preparation would take a great deal of time.

The ships for the journey needed to be built.

The immigrants selected and prepared for the trip.

The entire population would eventually need to migrate but there would need to be an order to the entire migration process.

The power generation units necessary to fold the space time fabric needed to be built as well. These units would need to be hundreds of times larger than the one on Maltar's scout vessel.

This again was a major challenge everyone supported but it all added to the preparation time.

All parts of the program were massive efforts and consumed the entire population and would consume most of the material of the planet.

There was little resistance but massive logistical challenges and problems all which slowed things down.

Maltar slowly consolidated his power. His political influence grew on a daily basis. He was elected as one of the Grand Marshalls of the realm. This made him one of the most powerful leaders of his time.

What he wanted he got.

He brought the members of his original exploration team along.

Most of his allies figured he would send someone else on the first colonization mission.

Maltar, however, always kept his personal goal of being first in establishing his people on a new planet in front of him.

He wanted to return to the blue jewel he had found with his team. His original team members knew he would be at the helm of the first ship to return to the planet they had found and to a person they knew they would be with him.

Maltar recognized the explorers returning with additional planets suitable for colonization.

None of the other planets were as beautiful or as bountiful as the one Maltar had discovered. These other planets were truly empty of intelligent life, most had only the beginning of any molecular activities. Several had the early development of life but no animals.

Life seemed to be rarer than the scientist had predicted and other intelligences even rarer. The variety of life from Caligria would need to be re-established on these other planets.

This would make their colonization a more complicated process than the one to Maltar's planet.

Maltar ensured the colonization for these habitable planets were planned and the ships for them were put in the building queue. He made sure all the migration ships necessary for the movement of all but a hand full of Caligrians would be built and ready to go within twenty cycles of his personal departure.

A small contingent of Caligrians would remain on the home planet and monitor the death of their star. Eventually, they too would leave. An automated monitoring station would be on Caligria to the end.

He ensured his project remained the primary focus. The time for the departure of the first colonist was finally set.

To the surprise of his many, Maltar resigned his post as Grand Marshall and accepted the post of Colonization Leader.

Maltar knew he would have supreme command in his new environment and the richest Caligrian Colony. He would ultimately influence and control the entire Caligrian Celestial Empire.

His thoughts were on the future.

He would later consolidate the Caligrians into a single confederation spanning the breath of the known Universe. He was not stepping down but stepping into the future.

It would be a future of his making.

Though Maltar was the mission commander and would call the shots on the how the colonization would proceed he had a social commander equal to his rank.

The social commander would be a strong influence on how the society established itself once on the planet. Maltar had worked hard to influence selection of the candidates for this position. He had been successful in eliminating the most fundamental religious leaders. He had wanted a social commander he could manipulate.

He did not get that wish.

Vesian had grown up with very traditional parents and had pursued the religious beliefs and practices long practiced by the Browns. Her education, beliefs and personal ambitions had moved her up the religious organizational structure.

Her willingness to try new ideas and her own concerted efforts had put her in charge of the religious wing of the colonization effort.

She was aware of Maltar's efforts to select the candidate he wanted.

Though she was friends with many of the candidates, she knew none were strong enough to counter a very ambitious Maltar.

She on the other hand, had her own influential friends in high places and leveraged them to make sure they supported her efforts to gain the position.

She wanted to make sure she would be the key voice in establishing the Caligrian culture in the new world.

As the religious leader she was of equal status to Maltar. She was slightly younger than Maltar and had been better known than he, until his heroic return from his exploration.

Vesian had decided on her course of action when she had heard the rumor of what Maltar had done to ensure his return to a planet that did not have intelligent life.

Though she understood his reasoning, she did not agree with his decision. She also felt the pressing need to get her people dispersed to other planets and did not bring up the issue of Maltar's previous actions.

Had she done so, she was sure the Caligrians would have lost the hero they needed at this time of great social upheaval.

Vesian was of the belief that the three distinctly different groups of Caligrians were equal in status. Even after thousands of cycles, the distinction between Blacks, Browns and Tans were still a cause for prejudiced behavior.

The Blacks had been the warriors and rulers. The Browns had been the religious and business leaders. The Tans were the workers and field hands. The current social order of the day sported an almost equal mix of the three in all fields. Equality was in fact practiced. Only the social behaviors still supported some of the past behaviors.

Maltar's leadership team showed no sign of any prejudice. It was clear to Vesian when she reviewed the selection; Maltar had in each case selected the best candidate.

In the selection of the colonists, Maltar was either very prejudiced or he was expecting trouble. Blacks made up half of the population. The Browns, Tans and mixed made up the remainder.

It was as if Maltar was anticipating a power struggle and wanted a higher proportion of the more aggressive blacks in the population of colonists.

Vesian was relieved to learn that more than seventy percent of the migrating population was religious. She hoped this would provide her with a balance of power. She would not be pushed aside or ignored.

Once on the planet, she would establish a government run by the people, not one controlled by a few powerful leaders. This would be the point when she and Maltar would most likely butt heads.

Maltar celebrated the day when the fold generators were tested for each of the transport vessels. These tests were brief and used to verify the generators were working.

The four enormous vessels were ready to load. The preparation and loading took almost a full cycle.

Each vessel held two hundred fifty million Caligrians and all the materials required for the establishment of the colonies.

Each vessel had its own crew and captain.

Each was in fact a small world onto itself.

Maltar promoted four of his team to be captains of the three ships. He was in command of all four.

Each of the ships had a contingent of twenty scout ships. Only one of these smaller ships had a fold generator. The remaining seventy-nine scout ships were to be used as local transport to and from the mother ships.

Once the colony was established on the planet, three of the transport vessels would return to Caligria to be used for transport to other planets.

This reuse had become a necessary part of the plan when the size and resource drain of building them was realized. The colony would be left with one transport vessel, nineteen regular scout ships and one scout ship with the fold capability.

Maltar looked around the command room. Half the room was holographic and actual people sat on the other half. Each of the four transport ship captains and their teams were in their own command rooms.

He addressed them and asked them if there were any last moment questions or issues.

There were no questions. There were plenty of last-minute problems, but they were minor and would be handled by the crew of each ship.

He looked around at his leadership team. His original exploration team members were all present. Each had left their own very successful careers to return with Maltar. Each remembered the thrill of having found a viable and fruitful new planet for the Caligrian population.

Vesian and her staff were sitting almost to a person opposite across from Maltar.

"Fold," was Maltar's single command.

And the fall began.

This time the crew knew it would be almost exactly a twenty-hour fall. They went about their normal duties until it was close to their arrival time. They knew to be seated in their impact seats a few minutes prior to the exit.

The entire ship had practiced their arrival positions. They would be laying down for the stop at the exit point.

"Fifteen minutes and counting," the computer sounded a warning.

Everyone went to their seats and strapped in.

The Hologram showed the blue planet and all four ships heard Maltar curse and cry out

"NO, it can't be,"

8 *Alien Appearance*

altar stared at the satellites, the transports between the two planets, the lights on the dark side of the planet and let out a groan as he sat down. He had immediately stopped his broadcast to the four ships. He was overcome by this unexpected situation.

Another group of beings had arrived before him.

He was online with his four Captains, his leadership team and with Vesian's team. They needed to come to grips with the situation and then proceed.

Maltar was inclined to settle on the planet in spite of the guiding principle to never interfere with intelligent life. He knew that no intelligent life existed on his prior visit.

Where had it come from?

It was apparent that the Caligrians were superior in technology.

The presence of the first alien ship was almost immediately spotted. Its' size and the flash of light preceding it were enough to make it quickly identifiable.

The materialization of three additional space vessels or small worlds was enough to alarm the entire Earth leadership.

The Worldwide Council requested the US President to lead and guide the interaction with the on-coming aliens.

Emma's prominent role in the scientific community and her work on the bending of time and space made her an immediate member of the Global team called together by the President. Her summons by the President surprised her.

This was not the first time she had been to the White House, but it was the first time to meet with the President and his leadership team. She walked into the security area and was greeted by one of the President's aides. After clearing security, she was taken to the meeting room where the President had convened a meeting of his top advisors.

Emma looked around the room and realized there were scientists, politicians, and the space management authority leaders in the room.

For the first time, she wished there still existed a military force, but it had ceased to exist many years earlier. She still remembered marching with the anti-military crowd as they pushed for the dismantling of the last vestiges of the three branches of the military.

So long ago, and so naïve, she thought. Now they were encountering aggressive aliens and were defenseless.

Emma became the focus for the communication between the Global team, the Worldwide Council, and the Aliens.

Signals were sent out.

Now here she was in the meeting with the President. Alien contact had been made. At least their presence verified. The messages sent out had not yet been returned. The Aliens were silently approaching, and the world was in a panic.

When she was shown the appearance of the aliens, she immediately recognized time travel in the manner of appearance of the spaceships. It had many of the same parallels to her work, but she was fighting to extract individuals and had no special movement capability.

The aliens, however, were capable of traveling with massive structures through their constructs. The power required to transport people across time was massive. She could only wonder at the power required to move the immense structures now coming toward the Earth.

The size and number of ships seemed ominous.

If they were here on a friendly mission, would they have come in such mass?

Would they have come in such huge ships?

Perhaps the size of their ships indicated they were of large size as well.

Emma conclude that the alien technology would be superior and if they had military power the people of Earth were doomed.

The President needed a plan. Emma participated in a round robin of discussion, demands for action, and cries of despair.

Emma was one of the key leaders to drive the group to take action. The decision to prepare for a confrontation was reached.

All space going vessels were called in for quick armament fitting.

A global military proposal was taken forward to the Worldwide Council.

Long dormant weapons production facilities were ordered to be reactivated.

A draft was established to staff an air and ground corp. They would be called the Space and World Armed Forces.

They were immediately called by their initials SAF and WAF.

The alien spaceships were approaching slowly almost as if hesitating to engage.

Emma led the team trying to establish communications with the aliens. Her team sent up multiple messages in an attempt to get some reply with which to work.

Simultaneously, Emma was keeping an eye to the upcoming extraction her other team was managing.

She returned to her extraction facility in the Yellowstone National Park.

She continued to participate with the Alien Tracking and Communication (ATC) team via the global net.

Emma now had two major teams she had to work with each day.

She was acutely aware that she and her colleagues had missed a gigantic portion of the mathematics of the space time continuum. She contacted several of her more talented associates and tasked them to review the mathematics and science of the space time continuum.

The Aliens were direct proof of some shortcoming in the current understanding by those on Earth.

She had learned to access the past but had not broken the barrier of bending the fabric of space to facilitate escaping the limit of the light speed travel barrier.

It was obvious by their appearance that the Aliens had figured it out.

Emma was awakened by her Alien Tracking and Communication team. She looked at the clock and realized it was three in the morning.

She let out a small groan.

"We are sorry to wake you so early, but the Aliens have sent their first message," her Worldwide team member said excitedly.

Emma figured the team had not gone to sleep.

Emma remained mentally quiet until she had a cup of hot tea in her hand. The she asked what the Alien communication said.

They want to know where we came from and how long we have been here. The communication was in English!

Emma thought about the questions. She contemplated the appearance of the huge vessels. The biblical story of Noah's Ark flashed into her mind.

She concluded that they had been to the Earth in the past and determined it was a prime colonization planet.

They had studied the planet on this approach well enough to send the message in English.

Emma was immediately worried and apprehensive.

Emma thought again about the question of where the people on Earth had come from.

She immediately knew the reply.

Ask them what they saw the last time they visited.

Ask them what star they call home.

Tell them we will share how long we have been here when we get their reply.

The team hesitated and asked if Emma was serious.

Emma replied that she was very serious and that the message should be sent exactly as she had dictated it.

She needed to know what they had seen on their first visit. This time frame might prove to be important. It would provide Emma with a space timeline and some clue how the aliens were bending time and space.

The Worldwide leadership were concerned about the communication but yielded to Emma and the communication team.

Emma went about the work leading up to the extraction, but she eagerly awaited the reply from the aliens.

She had requested the technical communications group determine which ship was directly communicating with Earth.

Emma received her reply an hour later.

The four ships were more or less in a square formation as they made their approach.

The lead ship was doing all the communication, but all the ships were communicating with each other as well.

The communications and linguistic folks were running all the intercepted messages through translation algorithms. They were keen on getting firsthand knowledge of the alien language.

"On my last visit huge animals roamed this planet. No intelligent life existed. I see no evidence of the creatures we observed at that time. We are a billion strong."

The reply send a chill through Emma. The alien had witnessed the age of the dinosaur. The reply also indicated the person replying had personally been here.

Emma estimated a life span similar to the one just achieved on Earth. It took about thirty seconds to extract people from Earth's past.

The aliens were able to move physically across the fold of time and space.

However, the aliens did not know how to measure the time between their folds.

They were novices. Much more advanced novices but novices none the less.

Emma worded her reply.

"We evolved on this planet and this star is our home star. We welcome your visit and inquire about your intentions and how we can peacefully meet your needs."

The rapidly returned reply was somewhat terse.

That is hard for me to believe. Our intention is to colonize the third and fourth planets of this system. We will gladly share them with you. How many are you?

Emma dictated her reply.

Your colonization is not accepted or welcomed. We will be glad to host your visit and discuss setting up trade and provide you with the resources for the return to your own system.

We are twelve billion.

The Alien reply was, "We come prepared to share our advanced technology."

Emma replied, "We welcome your offer of technology. However, we are not prepared to accept the movement of your people into our system."

Emma knew this last message would be the point at which the Aliens intentions became absolutely clear.

She was betting they would not leave. Even with their advanced capability she was sure they had expended a huge amount of their resources to migrate such a large number of what she was sure were colonist.

This was the Boston Tea Company and the Indians bargaining for the Island of New York only it was the Aliens and the Earthlings doing the bargaining.

Emma had no illusions at the poor and weak position the Earth found itself in.

This time the reply did not come back for more than six hours. Emma and her team discussed the meaning of the delay.

Emma pointed out the discussions that had gone on when the settlement of Mars was in the works. The philosophers had argued for the sanctity of the potential Martian organisms. Science fiction brimmed over with the protocol of advance civilization non-interference with intelligent life.

"Well, I hope the side not wanting to disturb us wins," one of the team members quipped.

Emma pointed to the picture of the four vessels. And asked the team to imagine the time, energy, emotional investment of a billion people and the energy required to launch them and cross the space time continuum.

Would you stop the effort? Could you?" Emma replied.

Finally, the reply came back.

"After much discussion we have concluded we will send half of our population to the fourth planet and half to the third planet. We feel this shows our goodwill in sharing the two planets and working in harmony with you."

Emma dictated her reply and asked that it get reviewed by the Worldwide Council before it was sent out.

Her reply was, "You have reached the wrong conclusion. The actions you are proposing are actions we will vigorously oppose. We include force and direct retaliation if you attempt to unload your people uninvited onto the surface of either planet.

Please study our history, we will invoke a burnt Earth policy in our battle against your aggression. Even with your superior technology, you will not settle on the Earth as you see it now. You will only inherit a burnt rock."

Her message was read and sent without any edits.

Emma hoped the aliens had a past of wars and strife and could identify with what she was communicating.

She asked to have the historic documentary war videos of the past beamed out to the spaceships.

Maltar was furious. Where these beings blind? Did they not understand the power they were facing?

He immediately ordered his team to develop a plan that would allow them to begin to send settlers down.

Their first two transports were forced by the Earth beings to crash land and the colonists were seized. The transports were immediately moved away from the landing location. It appeared they were taken underground.

Maltar called his team together and ordered them to prepare battle plans.

9 *Matt and Andrew*

arshal was touring the extraction facility with Emma. He was surprised to learn that she had been working on the Extraction program for one hundred years.

He asked how old she was and was surprised to learn Emma was one hundred forty-seven.

He complemented her on looking in her mid-forties.

He next inquired about the length of the Extraction program.

Emma circumvented the question by stating that the first successful extraction had been ten years ago.

Three people were successfully extracted and reinserted to some thirty thousand years into the past.

We have continued to refine the technology and to reduce the power required for the creation of the wormhole that makes the extraction possible. Even then the power consumption is enormous. You and Samantha almost took us over the limit.

I am sure Matt and Andrew will test our power limit again.

Emma then led Marshal into the extraction observation room. He asked if it would be possible to have a cup of tea or coffee.

He surprised her again by asking how the battle with the Caligrians was progressing. You gave the first black eye by downing and stealing their first two landing vessels, but you are now taking a beating from mama bear he continued.

Once again Emma was flabbergasted and asked how he was able to find out this information when her extraction team didn't know the facts.

Marshal smiled and promised to tell her in the near future if she was successful in extracting his two sons.

The control system announced that the extraction was about to commence. Marshal watched intently to see what he could learn.

Matt and Andrew hit the landing areas flat on their backs and swatted the surface the same way that he had. The impact caused them to bounce up and they landed standing in a defensive Tae Kwon Do position. They were both second degree black belts and at the moment they were confused and very defensive.

Matt immediately warned the suited figures to stand back.

Marshal wondered what the two had talked about on their way to the future.

He took his two sons in. Matt, the taller bulkier, more muscular of the two stood just a little over six foot three. Andrew was virtually the same height but was slender and lithe. Both sported well developed six packs.

He thought that in their present stance they would make great subjects for a nude drawing class.

He quietly spoke into what he took to be the equivalent of a microphone. So, you two naked ninja's are trying to look tough!

Matt replied that if this was one of his practical jokes, he and Andrew were going to kick his butt.

Marshal smiled and laughed. It would take more than two of you he replied as he grabbed the two outfits he saw on the counter and walked out to the receiving area.

He told each of them how glad he was to see them and gave them a hug.

Emma waited until the greetings were over and the two had a chance to put their suits on.

Marshall explained that in his case the extraction had been an accident.

He told Matt that Samantha was here as well.

Matt could only say wow.

Andrew asked Marshal why he was an accident. Did this mean their arrival had been planned?

Let's just say how happy I am to be here to greet you.

He worried about Nora, but he had already formulated a plan that he thought would take care of that end as well.

Andrew looked around and looked at Emma. He and Matt had speculated they had been falling through time.

He asked her, "When have we found our father?"

"I suspect we are still in the same place,"

He was looking around and taking in the technology around the room.

Emma was again surprised at the quickness of the new extractions. Matt was quietly observing her and the surroundings. He was not as outspoken, but he seemed to be penetrating and evaluating the situation.

She concluded that both of these new arrivals were at the top end of the IQ spectrum and like their father they were quick, direct and to the point.

Marshal had talked with Leslie, Emma's support and had arranged for a larger apartment for four people.

Emma was surprised at this request when she learned about it but pleased that Marshal was taking care of himself and now his family.

Now she understood why the request had been for a place with four bedrooms. Leslie had arranged to put them in two doubles with an adjoining door.

Marshal let Matt know that his future wife had arrived before him. He left out the fact that they had traveled time together.

"The young lady you were so enthralled with is here," Marshall said to Matt.

Marshal decided to take control of the situation and hasten the proceedings. He introduced Emma and explained her role and that she needed to get them examined and then he would lead them to their apartment. There he promised to fill them in on what he knew, and they could work together to see how they would be productive in this time.

As she walked along, Emma was listening to an on-going discussion by her team. She had escalated the issue up the chain of command to the top leadership.

Interest was very high in what the three knew. It was clear that the family as a whole represented a change in the quality of persons being extracted.

Several meetings with Marshal and his two sons were being planned.

Emma was intrigued by the three, in their ability to adapt to the situation so quickly.

Matt seemed to be the most thoughtful one.

Andrew seemed to be the quickest. Marshall was the most assertive and forceful.

This made sense to Emma since he was the father.

Marshal looked at Emma and asked if the team had decided what to do with the three of them.

He knew she was online with her team.

His team he said quietly knowing they would hear him

Andrew knew instantly what was going on. He said hello as well and that he looked forward to meeting them soon. He hoped he could be added to the team chat line.

Matt just wagged his head. He and Andrew had just been experimenting with a new app that simulated a team mental network. Now here in the future they were experiencing in directly.

They arrived at the apartment.

Marshal saw at once that this apartment was much nicer than the one, he had been in. Leslie was waiting for them and explained that Emma had upgraded the selection, and this was the only four bedroom in the entire facility. It was the executive suit for upper echelon and dignitaries.

Marshal smiled and gave Emma a peck on the cheek when he thanked her for being so generous.

He listened as Leslie launched into her explanation of how the room worked.

Marshal was not surprised with the ease that Matt and Andrew took to using the cube. In their own time they were web and app programmers and were constantly talking about programing in various languages. Marshal watched and listened to their chatter as they penetrated and accessed information on the cube.

Emma was stunned. The ease with which these two played with and penetrated the system was redefining what her team thought they knew about the people in earlier times.

Emma and her team watched as the two broke through several information barriers simply by trying different routes through the barriers and playing with various passwords and talking about back doors.

Clearly it was a simple game to them.

They quickly won once they figured out the construct.

Matt was especially good at breaking through the barriers on the net.

Marshall made a point of ordering some food for lunch.

He was planning to take the two for a tour of the facility.

He relaxed when Emma seemed distracted for a moment and then said that she needed to attend another meeting.

She and Leslie left together.

Emma left wondering what the three would do for the afternoon. Her team reassured her that they would keep an eye on the three.

They would be able to monitor the use of the Cube and the room had been set up with a camera system.

She saw that the three seemed to be in an intense learning mode. It seemed strange to her that the three were able to adjust so rapidly to the situation they found themselves in.

There was no, "How do we get back, or why us," kind of questions she had expected."

The living quarters had been prepared to observe the three. Her team was intensively interested in their actions and speed of learning.

She felt a little guilty for setting the three up for such observation, but it was part of her job.

She too felt there was something very different about the three.

Emma felt guilty about the camera system, but she justified it to herself in the light of the battle the world was in with the Caligrians

She was now hurrying to get to her meeting room to meet with the team trying to develop a battle plan they had evolved into a war strategy team.

Marshall had expected their new quarters to be "bugged." He made his initial round of the rooms and he spotted what he thought were the cameras or equivalent technology. He made a point of examining the artwork placed around the apartment.

These pieces of art were notable because his previous quarters had almost no art. He didn't incapacitate any of the monitoring devices, but he did reposition them.

He was repositioning each piece ever so slightly as he created a blind spot at the door area.

He also made a point of showing the art and pottery to Matt and Andrew.

He was pleased when each indicated they understood why he was showing them the art. The two picked up immediately on the purpose of the artwork.

Marshal asked Andrew to find some good music on the cube.

Andrew made the music suitably loud.

Marshal very quietly asked if the two could program a random conversation generator using the cube.

The conversation needed to be low and garbled but needed to seem real.

Matt gave a chuckle because he had written a talking head app and with the programing technology that he and Andrew had discovered available on the cube, the two would have one working in minutes.

Marshal relaxed and watched as the two worked with the system and then activated a game based on the questions generated from a random question generator.

It sounded as if one would ask a question and the other would spend time answering the question. It was quite ingenious. Marshall was impressed with the speed with which the two had set up the game.

Meanwhile he went about creating more blind spots in the video coverage. He wanted it to seem the room was occupied but that the video coverage had blind spots because of his rearrangement of the artwork.

He wondered how long it would take the observation team to catch on.

The lunch delivery arrived.

Marshall had shared how they would walk out with the person delivering lunch. Matt and Andrew carried on a quiet conversation as they escorted the young lady out and back to the people carrier.

The three carried the ordered lunch and rode the people carrier to the Old Faithful Lodge.

Matt and Andrew carried on a conversation with the young lady during their trip back to the hotel.

Marshal made the observation that the two were much better than he in extracting practical information on how to navigate around in their new environment.

Matt and Andrew made the observation that except for the people mover the park grounds appeared to have become wilder. They both also stopped to admire the lodge building and wondered if it was a replica or if it had somehow been preserved. The fact that it was still a National Park surprised all of them.

Marshal allowed the two a few moments to take in the seven-story high grand lobby and the dominant fireplace across from them.

Matt voiced the same sentiment, he had when he first came into the hotel, about wanting to go to his room to see if he was still checked in.

He saw that the cube that he had come to consider as his was vacant. He suggested that they get online and learn what they could about the Aliens.

He gave Matt and Andrew a quick update of what he had learned from his previous use of the cube.

Andrew learned how to search and organize a topic and soon they were pouring over everything that was on the cube.

Matt commented on how easy it was to search for information and that the system appeared to lack any security.

He listened as Andrew and Matt analyzed the information on the Caligrians. They were a long-lasting race that probably visited the Earth in the time of the dinosaur. This first visit was probably a scouting mission, and they were now returning with the intent to colorize and populate the planet.

Andrew pointed out that the communication between the Earth and the four spaceships indicated the Caligrian doing the communication had personally been on the first scouting mission.

This meant the Caligrians either had life spans in the millions of years or they had not yet figured out the relationship and effect of creating the fold in the timeline they were living and the timeline of the space they were folding.

Andrew went on to postulate that the more space that one were to fold the more the difference would be created in the time relationship between the two locations.

He envisioned the Caligrians building the huge ships after the return of the scout ship in a five-year period.

They had visited Earth sixty-five million years ago. Their star was in our universe but on the other side. They folded a lot of space. This would make one Caligrian year roughly equal to thirteen million years here on Earth. That of course did not make sense but if their time was roughly equal to Earth time then this fold had brought them to this point in time due to their inability to make the exact same fold in both the time and space continuum.

He and Matt quietly ate their lunch as Andrew postulated his theory.

Matt commented that what Andrew was saying made sense but the Caligrians were now taking aggressive action to colonize the Earth and were facing aggressive resistance by the Earthlings and Earth was not doing too well.

Marshal requested Matt to gather all the reports of the current battle with the Caligrians

This time Matt summarized what had been gathered. The Caligrians are a billion in number, their technology is superior to ours, they are no longer in a negotiating mood and have even claimed to be able to destroy the planet entirely.

Earth's defiant reply had been to let the Caligrians know that would be the only way they would successfully overcome Earth's resistance.

Matt waited until last to share that it appeared that Emma was the key person talking and negotiating with the Caligrians.

He was surprised, no he was shocked. He came to the conclusion that he had not given Emma enough credit for her huge mental capacity and capability.

He turned back to focus on the war effort and asked about Earths weapons.

After a few moments it was clear that Earth was out gunned and losing ground rapidly.

He asked Matt whether he could get into the system that controlled the facility in which they were staying. He explained the problem of their DNA being the key for all the doors.

Matt and Andrew both turned their attention to getting into the system. Matt quickly constructed a password cracking routine that allowed him to get into any location.

They linked all of their DNA into the system and gave all of them the highest clearance possible.

Andrew gave a small chuckle when he gave himself a clearance at the same level as Emma.

Matt commented on the fact that the system was so permeable that any information that was stored on it would be available to them with only a minor amount of hacking. He wondered if the Caligrians had been able to get onto the World-Wide Web.

Andrew concluded that if they were on the web, then they would know everything the people on Earth were planning.

This set alarm bells off for Marshal.

Andrew proceeded to pile on more concern by tying into the meeting Emma was attending.

He had figured out how to track and monitor any individual that he had the DNA signature for.

The three of them were the topic of the meeting Emma was in. This group wondered if the extracts, who came from a very warlike period would have any knowledge on how to effectively wage war.

Marshal commented that the situation must really be desperate if a global team was looking to them for help.

The global team gave Emma permission to grant the three full access to the information that might be useful in getting their help.

Hopefully, there is another layer or another secure system that holds the secret stuff. We have given ourselves all the access that is available on this system Matt said quietly.

Matt went on to state that the world needed a secure system. He could establish one on the current Worldwide.

He countered his own statement by pointing out that the Caligrians might have better hacking technology and better hackers.

Marshal saw the pizza delivery guy carrying the two pizza's he had ordered. He declared it was time to get back to the apartment and the three followed the pizza delivery guy to the people mover.

"Weren't you the one who delivered the pizza yesterday," Marshall inquired?

"Yeah, do you just want to take the pizza now," the young man asked.

"Thanks, but we'll let you formally deliver it. We don't want to take your job from you," Marshall replied.

He wanted to make sure they could get back in.

If Andrew had been successful, they would be able to get in without the help of the Pizza delivery.

He also wanted to use the pizza delivery as a distraction that would allow him to reorient the monitors in the room.

It seemed he would not need to continue this subterfuge, but it was always good to keep ahead of those trying to be in control.

Emma arrived at the apartment to find the three relaxing and eating pizza.

After a quick greeting Emma asked if the three were willing to review and give advice on the battle plans being developed to fight the Caligrians.

She watched the three as they all agreed that they would be pleased to get involved.

Emma made a point of letting them know how desperate the Global defense team was and that they were hoping to get some knowledge from the past that would help them in this current desperate situation.

Andrew offered Emma a piece of pizza. Knowing that she was multi-tasking two major and complicated issues he was looking at her with new respect.

Emma looked at the three and shared the radiation therapy and the chemical therapy the three would undergo on the following day.

She explained the radiation therapy would be done in a radiation booth that each would need to sit in for several hours. Their heads would stick out of the booths and they would be able to interact with an information cube and each other.

She asked if they were in agreement with this procedure.

Marshall looked around at Matt and Andrew to see it they were OK.

Emma was relieved none had any issues about the upcoming schedule.

"I think we will be OK with what you have planned. I am wondering if we will have access to the types of existing weaponry," Marshall inquired.

"I am wondering where Samantha might be and when I can meet her," Matt chimed in.

"Me, I was just wondering what you were doing Saturday night, and would you show me around the nightspots," Andrew added.

Marshall sat laughing quietly. He finally saw Emma loose her composure. She sat looking back at the three of them and was speechless for a few moments.

Emma was glad she had isolated herself before entering the apartment. Her team would have a field day if they had been part of the exchange going on.

As I mentioned yesterday to Marshall, we generally do not awaken any of those we extract, so Samantha is in one of the holding rooms.

I will arrange for you to have access to the information on weapons. And I would be pleased to show you around the night spots," Emma recovered and smiled at Andrew.

It had been quite a while since anyone had asked her out. She was probably four times older than Andrew, but she appeared like someone his age.

Marshall thanked Emma for getting them access to the existing weaponry. He was confident that Matt or Andrew could have gotten that information, but this opened the doors officially.

Emma was not sure what had just transpired but it was clear these three were going to have an impact.

Marshall seemed to have a clear idea of how to change the balance of the battle.

Matt had this uncanny ability to penetrate all systems. She was attracted to Andrew but there was something there that she did not yet have a handle on.

She was older than all of them, but she felt like a new tender foot. In a way if felt refreshing. Of late, the three were the only positive things to come her way.

Once Emma left, Matt looked at Andrew, "Wow, I have never seen you work so fast, and I am wondering why.

"Well, she is hot don't you think?" Andrew asked as he smiled back.

Matt replied that the extraction must have changed Andrew's attraction.

Marshal held his tongue. He knew Andrew was gay and was not attracted to Emma in a sexual way but more in a mental way. Andrew had recognized her as having a powerful mind and that dominated his perspective.

"Tomorrow we will press to have Samantha awakened. We are the only three ever to have come through awake. There must be something in our DNA that makes us different. I wonder what the difference might be. The others they have extracted have been sent back some thirty thousand years. The goal is to enhance the human species and accelerate the progress of the human race.

I personally wonder how many times this cycle may have been done before?" Marshall said looking at Matt and Andrew.

"Great question, how do they know what they have done in their future?

The future would probably put blocks in so the people in this time could not look forward. But perhaps we could skip significantly forward to a time not yet affected.

We could then determine if the Caligrians can be beaten or perhaps read history on how to beat them." Matt suggested.

Marshal suggested they concentrate on understanding the current situation firsthand, decided the actions they should take before trying to skip to the future for the answer they would first have to resolve in this time frame.

He would however keep the comment in mind as they investigated this time travel capability.

10 Samantha

mma found the three drinking coffee the next morning. She let them know that she had arranged to awaken Samantha in the late afternoon. She wanted to make sure the three of them were present when she did.

She pointed out the fact that the one extraction that had been previously awakened experienced a mental breakdown.

Marshal offered Emma a cup of coffee. He knew she was awakening Samantha because he had insisted. He had made it a condition of his help in developing a battle plan against the aliens.

She was losing a valuable reinsertion candidate.

Matt and Andrew reassured Emma that they would be there. Samantha had shared dinner with the three of them and they did not anticipate any issues.

"I hope we can connect this time as well as I think we connected that first evening," Matt said.

Emma then let Marshal know that the Global military planning team would arrive later that day or that evening and that the next day was scheduled for the three of them to participate in the battle plan review.

Marshal began listing the information he wanted to be available for the meeting. He requested a listing of all available weapons, a general understanding of where the battles were taking place and how information and communication was being managed.

He knew the team listening in via Emma's mental connection would begin immediately gathering and organizing all the information.

Emma realized Marshall was talking to her team as much as to her. She wondered how he knew she was not isolated. There must be some mannerism she projected when she was connected.

Marshall just smiled at her irritation. He didn't like the mind meld currently being practiced. He certainly did not want that type of connection. He did, however, know how to utilize it to his advantage.

After breakfast, Emma led the way to the conditioning facility. There he, Matt and Andrew got into what they would have described as old-fashioned steam bath chambers. These chambers however had no steam in them instead they sported a fill that form fit around their bodies. They had a sensation of being afloat in a pool or suspended in Jell-O.

Once they were situated in the conditioners, they turned their attention to the cube and began interacting with it.

Emma excused herself as she explained that she was off to set their calendars for the next several weeks. She shared that they would quickly realize they had landed in a tempest and that the people they would be working with were desperate. They were looking for a miracle.

"Be sure to come back before we become children again," Andrew called out after her.

Emma just waved her hand over her head as the door closed behind her. She was getting use to the challenging banter that came out of all the Samuels' family members.

Marshal suggested the review everything about the Caligrians that they could find on the Worldwide.

Matt called up the very first sighting and then set up a key word string to guide the cube.

If there is something you want to zoom in or study just say stop and give your command.

Matt worked for a few moments with the cube.

Marshal found it curious how well Matt could guide the cube to get it to do what he wanted. He had a keen sense of the logic being used to control the cube.

Meanwhile, Andrew began singing a song about a penguin.

"OK, OK, I'll hurry just get that song out of my head. I will be humming that for days," Matt said as he continued to set up his routine.

"There, now let's pay attention. It will begin in ten seconds,"

"Stop," Andrew said almost immediately.

The flash froze in its three-dimension view on the cube.

"Hey, it didn't even get... Oh," Matt began and then realized the view exposed something behind the flash.

"Tell me what the two of you see," Marshal said a little frustrated with not having a clue what he was supposed to see.

"Look through the hole behind the flash. You can see the stars in the region beyond. There are probably enough stars that we can find the galaxy our visitors are from. We need to get that view exploded and analyzed," Andrew said quietly.

Marshal instructed Matt to save the shot to several locations and to hide it across the net in as many places as possible.

He put a call into Leslie and asked her to bring a memory cube.

This he knew that image would be extremely valuable information. The location of where the intruders came from could be used to provide counter offensive intelligence.

Leslie arrived a few moments later with the requested memory cube.

Marshal asked Matt to put the information on and then disconnect the cube from the Worldwide.

He asked Matt and Andrew to make sure the information on the cube was secure. The two talked for a moment and then Andrew wrote a routine to encrypt the information on the cube and to lock the cube and only the information with the key code could be stored.

They continued on for several hours and stopped several times to capture and save some key shots.

He noted that all the field battles were being won by the Caligrians. The Caligrian portable force field shields protected their fighters very effectively.

He was the one who spotted the fact that the shields did not protect the fighters from above.

He had Matt save several of the battlefield pictures.

He pointed out the fact that the Caligrians were not very good at the battle they were waging. They seemed liked regular people versus soldiers.

Marshal made the comment that they seemed as green as the Earthling troops. They just have better technology on their side.

Emma came in exactly at noon and declared that the three were as young as they would ever get and that it was lunch time.

Emma waited out in the hall as the three got dressed.

Andrew teased Matt about the fact that he looked like he was twelve and that Samantha would never recognize him.

"Well, I am glad you will be with me because you look just as ugly as you did when she saw you last," Matt shot back.

He chose to ignore both his sons and asked what Emma had in mind for lunch.

He was not sure what the conditioner had accomplished so far. He did not feel any different.

"How about fish and chips? Is that something you would have eaten in your day," Emma asked as she led the way to the eating lounge.

He asked whether a cube could be taken offline and used independently.

Emma assured him that was possible.

Marshal gave the small memory cube with the critical information to Emma. He told her about the star system that could be seen through the hole as the Caligrians came through the fold. He made her promise that the memory cube would only be activated on an isolated system.

Emma's team heard the instruction and a few moments later Leslie arrived to collect the cube.

Marshal made a point of telling Leslie to have some astronomers identify the star system visible through the hole.

He also ordered a wall size poster of the hole.

Leslie declared that it was time for all of them to go and awaken Samantha.

The four were standing around Samantha as she was slowly brought out of her controlled sleep.

Marshal stood on her right and Matt to her left. Andrew was on the end with Emma. Samantha slowly opened her eyes and looked around.

"You, you fell off in front of me," Samantha said hoarsely to Marshal.

She looked at Matt, "What are you doing here? Am I in the hospital?" Who are you two?

Marshal handed Samantha a class of water.

Yes, you and I took a trip through time.

He pointed to Andrew and Matt and told Samantha they had taken the same trip.

Samantha responded that she had no idea what he was talking about. She looked under the sheet covering her and she asked why she had no clothes.

Marshal pointed to Matt and said he would explain everything while the rest of them stepped out.

Marshal led the three out of the room.

He told Emma that Matt would handle Samantha. Later we can see if there are any issues with Samantha coming out of her sleep.

He asked Emma to arrange for an appropriate and functional wardrobe for Samantha.

Later in the afternoon after getting the analysts kicked off on the photo analysis, they arrived back to the room where Matt and Samantha were still talking. It was clear the two had bonded and were comfortable with each other.

"Well, have you gotten over the shock yet," he inquired?

Samantha looked at him with a smile and declared that this was better than getting attacked by an old man while running on the ridge trail as she had expected.

She admitted to having trouble believing anything like this was possible. She really needed to get out and see it for herself. She felt like she was in the Twilight Zone.

She was happy Matt was with her. He had been on her mind when she went jogging. She had gone out jogging specifically in hopes of running into him.

She had not expected what was now becoming more believable to her.

As she listened to the chatter of the four people around her bed Samantha thought about how lonely she had been for the last few years.

She had lost both parents when their single engine plane crashed into a mountain side in Idaho. She had been in her last year of getting her Forestry degree. That year she buried both her parents. Her father had been raised in an orphanage and her mother was an only child.

Her grandmother was in failing health and suffered from Alzheimer's. Her grandfather had passed away the year before.

She was by all accounts totally alone.

She took a job as a forest ranger in her home state of Oregon. She was not so sure it was a good job for her. The beauty of the forests and the mountains was soothing to the soul, but the isolation was heavy on the heart.

She had chosen to go to Yellow Stone for vacation. She had contemplated going to Hawaii, or on a cruise to Alaska but for some reason Yellow Stone won out.

She told her friends it was a busman's holiday.

Now as she looked at Matt, and said she was glad she had gone.

She had, however, traveled much farther than she had anticipated.

Samantha looked around the room and then asked if there was any chance of getting to see something other than the inside of the room.

Emma nodded and suggested they go back to the apartment and get Samantha situated in her room.

Matt suggested dinner at the Old Faithful lodge at the same table that the family had first met Samantha.

11 Battle Analysis

The dinner at the lodge was a resounding success. Samantha noted that the park had been restored to more of its natural state. She and Emma discussed the efforts to restore Earth to a state that nature intended.

Andrew commented that time had improved the dinner menu.

Marshal sat quietly and absorbed the situation and once again thought through his solution to his own predicament.

It was late in the evening when they all returned to their apartment at the extraction facility.

Emma reminded them that the next day was scheduled for them to meet with the Global Battle planning group.

The next morning Emma came by to guide them to the meeting room. he, Matt, and Andrew had come to the conclusion that both sides were exceptionally poor at planning their battles and they could not determine the strategy being followed on either side.

Earth was in a life-or-death struggle and the planners seemed to be working on compromise plans.

He wanted to take over immediately but chose to spend the day listening to the team before initiating his own approach.

It turned into a long day for him. With Emma there were thirteen members of the Global War planning group. This group had been selected to represent the global government and key functional offices.

Managing crisis had been the normal activities of this team. Now they were chartered to manage the war with the Caligrians.

He concluded that they were not very good at battle strategy or tactics.

The meeting ended and he suggested they return to their apartment, order dinner and review what they had learned.

While they waited for the dinner delivery, they discussed and reviewed what they had listened to and heard throughout the day.

He gave Matt, Andrew, and Samantha the challenge of coming up with some out of the box battle strategies.

He, Matt, and Andrew viewed and reviewed almost every moment of every battle. They discussed the field shielding and how to counter this advantage.

They asked that any captured shield should be studied, and reverse engineered and issued to the Earth troops.

Marshal had paid close attention to the small ships supporting the Caligrian ground troops. Earth's aircraft were no match for them. There was no air support for the ground troops on his side.

When he learned that two of them had been captured and were in hiding, Marshal put them into the reverse engineering line up as well.

The following day Marshal asked about the actions taken directly against the Caligrian spaceships. He was shown a video of several missiles exploding well away from the ships.

The Caligrians had shield capable of stopping missiles and other projectiles. After firing several missiles at the giant ships, it became clear an attack on the main ships was beyond Earth's capability.

The smaller alien ships also had the same shielding system and they in addition had missiles and lasers that could take out any plane or spaceship Earth could launch against them.

Earth's planes and spaceships were brought in and hidden. The hope was to figure out a way to improve these resources so they would have a fighting chance.

Matt was the first to come up with a novel way to outwit the Caligrian shield technology. The shield appeared to evaluate the object approaching it. The smaller Caligrian ships probably had a code enabling them to get through the screens protecting the larger ships. Each of the smaller ships had their own shielding

Matt proposed transmitting something that would not trigger the shielding defense into the space inside the vessel.

He showed the them a matter transmitter that could be focused on a target area. Matter could then be transmitted into that area.

Matter transmission had just been developed in the last year and there were only two matter transmitters in existence.

Marshal groaned as he put another technology into the must do immediately list.

He congratulated Matt of coming up with one good idea and asked if there were any other ideas.

Andrew pointed out the way the shields were being used. He suggested launching projectiles in a high arc that would then come down from overhead. When the Caligrian soldiers raised their shield to protect, themselves a barrage of explosives throw at their feet would create havoc.

Marshal liked that idea even though a good field commander would be able to counter the situation by having only half of the shields raised for protection from the air. Since he thought the Caligrians were new to warfare it might take them longer to counter act this kind of attack.

Andrew made a good point of having it be part of a charge by Earth's soldiers.

Marshal put the idea on the list they were developing.

Samantha made the point that the Caligrians would quickly figure out how to counter act the matter transmitter. Once they figured out what we are doing they might be able to block all subsequent efforts. She suggested that all the ships should be hit at once and with as overwhelming fashion as they could make it.

He agreed immediately and thanked Samantha for pointing it out. He then suggested the attack should be focused on the giant transport ships. Specifically, they would want to target the ships control room.

Emma asked whether she should send this learning to her team.

Almost in unison the four shout NO!

Marshal looked at Emma. He asked Matt to call up the shot of the Caligrian ship coming out of the fold in space. He asked Emma what she saw.

It took her a moment then she looked at Marshal in astonishment.

The picture had been altered and the star system they had seen was gone.

Marshal made the point that the World-Wide Web was being monitored by the Caligrians.

He pointed out that Matt and Andrew had been able to get in and get full access to everything before Emma had granted it.

Andrew suggested they hack into the Caligrian communication and control system so Earth could know what they were up to. He pointed out that in Matt, the world had the best hacker in five hundred years.

Samantha asked how much power would be needed to transmit the amount of material they would need over the distances they were talking. She asked if the transmission had to overcome the gravity well the Earth represented.

Marshal looked at Samantha with new respect. He commented that he thought that she had majored in Forestry.

Suddenly it a plan became clear to him.

Marshal pointed to the fact that to date Earth had been on the defensive. The Caligrians were pushing Earth's defenders inward from all sides. He calculated that in about another thirty days the defenders would be positioned in four large groups. They would then be susceptible from an attack from the four ships.

He pointed out this trap to the group.

The ground forces had to stop retreating and go on the offensive.

Marshal asked Emma to convene all the Global Leaders in a location that could be totally isolated form the World-Wide Web and that could be isolated from a direct probe by the Caligrians.

He made the point that the Caligrians knew everything the Earth had been planning and doing from the very beginning.

It was time to change the situation and take extreme offensive action.

Marshal asked it the world still had a hard-wired communication system.

Emma replied that she did not know but that they could use couriers to carry the information.

Emma led the way to the meeting with the Global Battle Team members.

He asked if any of the team members were connected to the World-Wide Web.

Without saying a word, he wrote on the white board that he had insisted be part of the meeting, "Please disconnect. Let me know when each of you has done so."

One of the team members said he could not tell them to do it.

He refused to answer any questions. When two of the members refused to do so until he explained, he signaled to Matt and Andrew to escort the two out of the room.

He wrote on the board, "We are being monitored by the Caligrians who have full access to the World-Wide Web."

He thanked the team.

He signaled to Matt, Andrew and Samantha and left the room.

Emma was caught by surprise. She looked around at the Battle Planning team and knew immediately that Marshal would not work with them again.

She announced the meeting was over and rushed out of the room to catch up with Marshal.

She caught up with the four and asked Marshal if he needed a cup of coffee.

Marshal knew that Emma was desperate to get a plan that would win the war against the Caligrians. He also knew that he would no longer work with the team he had just left. It was time to escalate this to the top.

He asked Emma if she was isolated from the Worldwide. When she confirmed she was, Marshal then accepted offer for a cup of coffee.

Marshal voiced his concern about the lack of strategic thinking by the team she was leading. The fact they could not see that their armies were being herded into killing zones. He pointed out that the lack of team discipline was plain to see in how the armies were performing in the field.

Emma was stung by his harsh evaluation. She was surprised at the thoroughness of his planning and the hard stand he was now taking.

She suddenly realized why he had remained so composed when he had first arrived.

He insisted they gather the world leaders responsible for the war effort in a place where they could not access the Worldwide. He wanted total isolation. The only communication would be voice to ear and what was shared visual in real time.

He declared there would be no more meetings until everyone gathered in this safe location to develop war winning plans.

He insisted that couriers go out to all the world leaders to inform them that they should stay off the Worldwide system.

He asked that until the meeting, the Worldwide should be flooded with trivia about the battles being waged. The newscasters should broadcast how Earth's armies were driving the Caligrians back and how poorly the Caligrian fighters performed. He pointed out that nothing had to be real, just well written with enough visual footage to make the case.

He knew Emma was taking what he was saying badly. She seemed on the verge of getting mad. He knew she had worked hard and was trying to guide the Global Battle team as best as she could.

Andrew knew his father had gone into the control mode. There would be no give in the position he had just taken. He asked a question so they could hear the answer as a group.

"You are being very hard and critical. Do you think the world leaders will respond in a positive manner?"

Marshal understood the point of Andrew's question. He pointed out that there was one very narrow window of time in which they could operate and expect to win.

The five of us, sipping our coffee, have the ideas, concepts, and a way that Earth can win this war.

Emma must convince the right leaders to gather. She must use her connections to make this happen. If she can make this meeting happen, she will have done as much to win the war as the rest of us.

He watched as the look on Emma's face turned from being mad, to being determined. He would thank Andrew later for the question he purposely asked.

Emma excused herself and told them she would meet them back at their apartment.

He thanked Andrew for his question.

"Well, I hope they don't take too long to capitulate to you. They are taking substantial losses on a daily basis. Even with Earth's almost ten to one population advantage, the fighters are getting demoralized by being slaughtered like cattle," Andrew said with concern.

Emma returned almost an hour later.

"I have arranged for the isolation room you asked for. In fact, it is an isolation area. We will have to travel to it. We will leave this afternoon and go by high speed to Mount Yuka. There we have an absolute isolation room," Emma informed the team.

I have pulled every string and called in every favor I had outstanding and made some promises that I will not be able to deliver.

The President has signaled his support and would like to talk with you.

"Is there still a United States and is he the President you are talking about?" Marshal inquired.

"Yes, you will see him on the cube. He will be able to see you the same way. You will be on the net," Emma continued.

She hoped Marshal would not refuse.

"Alright, is he aware of the openness of the net," Marshal asked.

"Yes, I sent a cube by courier with the advice that nothing critical is to be shared," Emma replied.

Marshal looked around at the four and declared that they were a team, and they would talk to the President as a team.

After the greetings between the two, he introduced each of the people standing around him.

You of course know my very good friend and one of the most brilliant scientist in the world, Emma Gsyckiv. Next to her is Samantha Reading a top Forest Ranger in her day. Matt is my oldest son and Andrew is his younger brother both who are smarter than their father.

The conversation was cordial, and the President was really quite good at not divulging any information but making it clear his people would cooperate.

"I understand you are having an interesting time on your vacation. Some of my friends will be out that way. They will join you and I hope all of you have a good time. They are eager to go hiking with you and learn the climbing techniques you are famous for," the President replied.

What he was probably asking for was a review by his generals and other military leaders.

The communication ended.

Marshal turned to Emma and verbalized the message he had heard the President state.

Emma confirmed that the President saying that the people that would be at the meeting would listen and were looking for his guidance.

I know every top military leader will be there. Also, every top political operative will also be there.

Emma pointed out the five of them were now on center stage, in the spotlight and everyone attending would be wondering what they would sing and how they would dance.

Showing the President and other world leaders the photo shopping of the picture of the Caligrians coming through the fold convinced them they should listen to you.

Losing ground so steadily and realizing none of their systems are secure has all of them deeply concerned.

"Well, they should be alarmed. It is really going to be difficult to win battles when the enemy knows exactly what you are going to do, and they have advanced and maybe superior technology.

He reiterated that they should be concerned.

Winning the coming battles would cost the world dearly. They would need to overcome superior technology.

The price would be paid in the loss of life.

He asked Emma about the experience of the average fighter.

Emma informed the team that the fighters were all volunteers that had been activated upon the arrival of the Caligrians.

Emma explained that The United Nations became the global government and all nations contributed to a common support organization similar to an army. There had been no wars for over a hundred years.

The military structure of the world existed but its purpose was to provide support and assistance to address problem situations caused by nature.

We had no significant weapons when the Aliens arrived. In fact, almost everything being used to fight with was recently manufactured.

This relief organization was transformed into the fight force. The leaders are great managers but know nothing about battle strategies.

Marshal pointed to Andrew and gave him the responsibility of working with the leaders to develop their battle strategy.

They all left to get on the transport to the meeting area.

Along the way, Samantha commented on the wilder terrain than back in their time.

Emma commented that it had looked much the same through her lifetime. She speculated that a few hundred years of time would give them a very different comparison.

Samantha commented that she would love to work with the Forest Service to continue the restoration work.

They arrived in Jackson Hole and transferred to an underground people mover.

Marshal found it hard to believe they were moving at more than three hundred miles per hour in an underground floating train. The ride was so smooth it was hard to believe you were moving.

As they got out of the people mover, Matt asked if the Yuka Mountain facility was in fact the nuclear dump site from his time.

Emma confirmed that it had become the center for an Army Strategic command. It later became the place Congress would evacuate to in case of a nuclear war or major disaster affecting the Eastern seaboard.

It was reactivated when the Caligrians arrived. Currently most of it was not on the World-Wide web.

Marshal pointed out that this was a good thing because the Caligrians would not consider it an important site.

He went on to make the point that keeping them away from their information would be the best weapon available.

He was beginning to wonder how far down into the ground the Yuka site went when Samantha asked how far down, they were going.

Emma responded with the fact they would be on the bottom most floor. There was one more equipment level below this level.

Matt had skipped breakfast and was now ready for a good lunch. He asked whether there was a chance that this place had a restaurant or cafeteria.

Emma stepped off the elevator and was greeted by a very handsome young man in an army uniform. Emma guessed he was a lieutenant or perhaps one rank higher.

He asked if they were the Yellowstone team.

"Yes, we are," Emma replied.

"I am Lieutenant Alton Macpherson. I will be your guide while you are here. I will take you to the meeting room and then I am to take you to lunch. I have been instructed to have you back in the meeting room by thirteen hundred." Alton said saluting and shaking hands with each of them.

He then turned and said, "follow me," and walked briskly down a wide hall to the right of the elevators.

Marshal looked at the rest of the team and signaled with his hands to follow.

He would use the lunch period to get the team ready for the upcoming meeting.

12 Rise of the Phoenix

arshal followed Emma into a huge meeting room. The Yellow Stone team was sitting on a curved platform about a foot above the main floor. They were bookended with two information cubes that double the size that they had been using. It projected in three dimensions.

Marshal asked Emma to verify that these information cubes were isolated from the Worldwide.

Emma checked and replied that she had been assured that this floor and forty floors above had no Worldwide connection.

Marshal looked around at the people sitting at the circular tables. He told the team to stay put as he walked out into the meeting room and introduced himself. He shook the hand of everyone in the room. He surprised the servers delivering drinks and snacks to the tables by chatting with them as well.

Marshal was counting on the attendees getting restless. He wanted to get their real responses not the canned political double talk they had come prepared with.

It had been hard to gauge the age of those present. It was clear each of the important or primary representative from each country had several aids or supporters.

Marshal wanted only the decision makers in the room.

Emma stood up, introduced the Yellow Stone Team, and explained the role of each member.

She introduced him last.

"Marshal Samuels will provide an introduction, share the objectives of this meeting and will be the person that will lead the world to a victory against the Caligrians."

He stood up and thanked everyone for reacting so quickly to the short notice.

He looked around the room and said nothing for a count of twenty.

Then he asked the decision makers from each country or organization to stand up. He watched as about a third of the room stood up.

He then asked those that remained seated to please leave the room.

This caught everyone, even the Yellow Stone Team by surprise.

Emma looked at Marshal and thought better than to ask what he was doing.

She looked at Matt and Andrew who each raised one eyebrow in the same manner that Marshal did when he wanted to indicate either agreement or amazement. Emma was not sure what the two were now indicating.

She was in a state of shock.

Marshal repeated his request when their seemed to be a hesitation.

He made it clear that only the decision makers were to stay in the room.

Once the room emptied, he once again went to each table and gave a white sheet of paper to the persons remaining.

He then returned to the stage.

Ladies, Gentlemen, and those who like me are concerned and scared as hell. We have the fate of the world in our hands. The Earth is on the verge of being defeated by the Caligrians.

We on this platform are ready to guide you to develop the winning strategy and plans, and to go to the field to ensure our fighters begin winning and defeating our enemy.

I will now check to see that each of you has the required IQ to contribute to this winning plan.

Please fold the paper I gave each of you in half as I am doing.

Yes, you at this table do it too, Marshal said as he looked at Matt.

Now take the marker given to you by the caterers and print your name on each side as I am doing.

173

He wrote his name on his sheet and then waited a moment until the majority had printed their name.

Now, with the name side down fold each edge to the middle.

Fluff it out and put it on the table facing me.

Marshal took a moment to walk quickly out into the table area. He pointed around to each table.

He came back on stage and declared everyone competent to participate in saving the world.

He then started to clap, and everyone joined in.

By this time Emma was almost to the point of laughing.

He had just cycled the entire world decision making participants through anger, confusion, and a successful coordinated effort.

He had demonstrated total control of the situation.

Marshal explained that four of the Yellow Stone participants were from more than five hundred years in the past.

He made the point that they were culturally barbarians as compared to those from the current time. He shared his experience in two wars as a gunner and a field commander. He made it a point to state that he knew how to kill and that he had seen many killed.

He pointed out that there was no glory, there were no heroes. There were only those who lived and those who died.

The other three at the table have not bloodied their hands on the battlefield but they grew up watching and emotionally dealing with the violent world they lived in.

He paused as he looked around the silent room.

Then reintroduced each member on the stage.

Matt, a genius in at writing code hacking programs is amazed how open the World-Wide Web is to someone like him. Within two hours of his arrival, he was able to grant me the highest security clearance in the world. He will hack into and let us see what the Caligrians are doing.

Andrew with a powerful intellect and ability to dissect every situation and the keen eye that saw the Caligrian system through the fold will guide each of you in establishing a winning battle strategy.

Samantha, fundamentally the most refined of us four, always asks the probing question that causes us to improve what we have developed. She will review, critique and challenge what the participants in this room come up with.

Finally, a person of your time. Emma Gsyckiv, leader of the Global War Battle planning team will provide the guidance to all of us for the next several days.

Emma stood and walked to center stage.

"Let me share the agenda and then each of you will have five minutes to introduce yourself and to state your objectives."

Emma stopped as the doors in the back of the room opened. The room fell quiet as the President of the United States walked toward the stage.

Emma greeted President Johnson and accepted his hug.

"I made this trip so I could address this gathering in person. I have talked with leaders around the world, and they would like me to convey for them the critical nature of the success of this meeting. I implore you to listen, learn and to develop a plan leading to a victory for our side.

Emma assures me we can win if we employ the right actions. She has a team who will lead you to determine and plan the right actions. We are out of time. This is the time to act. You must come out of this meeting with a plan to win. Give it your all. Thank You," the President said as he left the podium and walked toward the door.

"Well, thank you Mr. President," Emma said as she again took the podium.

Let's begin our introductions.

Marshal listened carefully to each of the participants. He was especially interested in age and experience.

Each of the four on stage had been given the round robin assignment to capture the individual information of each decision maker. They were also to give their perception of the individual as to their ability to make solid, hard decisions.

Andrew took the first person, Samantha the second, Matt the third and Emma the fourth.

Once again Emma was surprised at Marshal's hands on approach. Everything they were doing was available on the World-Wide Web, but the hands-on approach created a powerful dynamic connection to these individuals.

Marshal again thanked everyone for attending.

He then called for a brief break.

During the break Emma informed him that the President wanted to speak to him personally.

Marshal went over to where Matt and Andrew were sitting and got them to agree to share their information when the meeting reconvened.

He would rejoin them after lunch.

Andrew took the stage and shared the discovery of the stars as viewed through the hole the giant ships came through. A group of astronomers were able to identify the star system out beyond Alpha Centuri that the Caligrians came from.

Emma in her initial communication with the Caligrians was able to determine that they had visited the Earth some sixty-five million years ago. The time it took them to prepare to come back ready to colonize the Earth was probably five to twenty years.

They were expecting to find the same wild animals, but they found us instead.

They did not and perhaps still do not know the incredible time that has passed since their last visit.

A person in the middle of the room raised the question as to why they attacked Earth?

And how does knowing the information just shared provide any help in winning the war?

At this point, this is part of getting to know and understand the enemy Andrew answered.

The ability of the Caligrians to fold time and space and transport a billion people through it means that Emma and her team, as brilliant as they are, missed a key part of the Space, time fold mathematics.

The Caligrians seem to know how to return to their launch time. This means they can do the equivalent of time travel.

For us this would mean we could go through the same portal visit them in their time and return back and still be in our time. This means we would be stepping back and forth in time and space. It is the knowledge that removes the limit of the speed of light for our ability to explore the Universe.

We are very close to directly having this capability.

Emma and her team is taking this new insight and revisiting their developmental equations and assumptions to see where they deviated from the space travel portion of our current extraction capability.

I am proof that she has been able to fold time and go back and extract people long dead in our context of life and death.

Emma does not know how to travel across this fold in time.

I share this only to show we are close to having the same technology as the Caligrians. They also have the ability to generate a tremendous amount of concentrated power to create the fold and to move objects as large as their transports.

Knowing that we are almost in the same place as the Caligrians should give us the confidence to understand and overcome any advantage they have.

Marshal rejoined the meeting as Matt took the stage.

Matt announced that he had been able to hack into the Alien equivalent to the World Wide Web. He had installed what he called hooks for later use.

He would lead a group of hackers and attempt to get into the alien control center.

This would give everyone the ability to see the Caligrian battle plans and to figure out how to beat them.

Matt sat down. Some in the room started clapping and the entire room followed.

"I would like to spend a few moments capturing what each of you thinks success is for this meeting. Then we will call it a day." Emma declared from center stage.

The suggestions came up on the cube as each person responded.

The session ended and the team, led by Alton, their assigned guide, led them to dinner in the cafeteria.

Marshal noted that Andrew and Alton were into a long discussion. It seemed they were connecting on a personal level.

The next morning Emma called the meeting to order and reintroduced Marshal.

Marshal asked the meeting participants to recall the previous day. He praised and thanked them for the culture of world peace and harmony they had established.

He stopped for a moment and stepped off the platform and in a loud voice shouted, "but you are pathetic at defending the human race from annihilation."

"You would be dust had you been fighting my army and I am the least of the soldiers of my time."

Marshal turned and came back on the raised platform.

He turned and quietly address the group.

Luckily, we are facing the Caligrians who were not expecting to wage a major battle. Their army is as green as ours. I read their early hesitation as disagreement on their side about the action they are taking. If we were Caligrians, the disagreement would have been about their right to interfere with our planet.

They are using their superior technology to herd our fighters into four killing zones. Once our fighters are bunched together, they plan to use their laser cannons to eliminate them. You are fighting their war and losing.

It is clear you have not studied the major wars and battle histories of the nineteen, twentieth and twenty first centuries.

Your armies are on the verge of annihilation.

Marshal stopped to get the reaction of the meeting participants.

He asked Emma to capture the questions and reactions.

He walked back onto the platform and took a sip of water and scanned the room.

The clamor in the room was loud and their seemed to be many excuses why Earth was not doing better. It was also apparent there were several participants who were just plain mad.

After about ten minutes, Marshal stood up and walked to Emma and thanked her.

He had gotten what he wanted.

The people in the room wanted action.

They wanted to win.

Emma called the meeting back to order. Marshal stood not saying a word until the clamor died down.

"I will get even for that," Emma whispered as they passed each other.

Marshal asked the audience if they had heard what Emma just said.

The room went quiet.

She is going to get even with me for putting her on the front line!

You will need to be mad, and you will need to get even with the Caligrians for the many men and women they have already killed.

But you will be putting many more soldiers on the front lines. You will wish they could all come back mad at you, but many will come back to you dead.

You are going to honor those you send to die by defeating the Caligrians.

Let me tell you how.

First our armies will stop retreating no matter what the cost in lives. If we must, we will send a constant stream of bodies into the battle until we over run them with bodies. Long ago this was how China beat the US army in Korea. Gun barrels melted but their armies kept moving forward.

We will do the same.

If this cannot be agreed to, then we need to all go home to our families and let them know we are going to turn over leadership of the Earth to the Aliens.

Is there anyone in this room who cannot agree to this?

"How are we going to stop them when we can't seem to stop their army's forward progress," the question came from one of the more irritated participants.

"Great question, thank you."

The answer is we just refuse to move and since I don't agree with suicide, we surprise the oncoming army with a new way of fighting and some new weapons.

Matt, Andrew, and I have analyzed their use of shields and have come up with a way to disrupt their effectiveness.

We will shoot shrapnel dispersing mortars to the back of the line. Simultaneously we shoot just below the shields to the front with fifty caliper machine guns armed with soft copper explosive bullets. This will create a shrapnel curtain at ground to knee level. At the same time, we will drop liquid napalm down randomly from above. Even with their shielding there will be a tremendous number of casualties. This will work only a few times before they learn to again shield themselves.

He then stopped and again stepped out into the room.

Then in a quiet voice he described the next horrific variation of the fighting tactic.

Hundreds of times worse than the shrapnel, we will use liquid napalm fired from napalm cannons.

Our action must be massive and must be coordinated. We will take this action on all battle fields at the same time. We will surge forward with twice as many men as we currently have on the field and we will do it on every battlefield simultaneously.

This is how we will stop and totally annihilate their ground threat.

Marshal looked around and then heard.

"How will we counter their air support as we make this mighty surge?"

"Yes, what are you going to do about their air support," he quietly repeated?

He scanned the room and counted to twenty.

That question leads me to ask Matt to describe how he plans to utilize a new technology.

Matt stood up and walked out to where he was standing. He was at least two inches taller than his father and had walked out to make use of this visual comparison.

He looked around and simply said that the Caligrians would be given the Earth they were fighting so hard for.

We are going to give them the earth until they capitulate and surrender. They will receive this earth in a manner they were not expecting to get it.

The first use will be against the ground support craft. Then we will do something similar to the giant transport ships. The details of how to do this is on the agenda for the breakout work sessions. You in this room will define this winning attack.

Our matter transmitters will transmit a fine, dusty, extremely dry dirt. We will spice it up with all the hottest ground red pepper this world has to offer.

They will surrender or suffocate in their vessels.

Matt looked around at the room and then told his father he had the floor.

Marshal thanked Matt. He turned to Emma and smiled.

He told the participants it was time to get to work.

He made the point that they had no choice but to win. They were to find all the barriers to a winning outcome and devise and execute the counter measure. He told them to utilize all the resources the world had in order to win.

He returned to his seat and sat down.

The room burst into a round of applause.

He noted that even the most ardent doubter in the middle of the room stood and applauded.

The meetings continued for the rest of the week. Each day the learning and progress was shared among all participants.

Each day a cube with the learning went to the President by courier.

A noticeable change took place in the atmosphere and attitudes of the participants. It was as if each day they ate another helping of self-confidence.

By the end of the week, he closed the meeting to a roaring, "We are going to win" chant.

The team planning the use of the matter transmitters identified the time required to produce the transmitters and tying them into the power system as a huge barrier.

Andrew took the responsibility to manage a crew of twenty thousand workers that would build two hundred massive matter transmitters. These would be built at two hundred of the largest power plant units in the world.

He recruited Alton and the two became inseparable as they traveled the world to coordinate the effort without the use of the Worldwide web.

They had only one month to pull it off.

The two hundred sites were strategically located to ensure that all the power available in the world could be routed to power the transmitters simultaneously.

Andrew slept during the high-speed transit by train. He thanked Emma for having insisted on getting them to use the conditioning booth.

Matt continued his work on breaking the Caligrian language and getting more control of their internal environmental systems.

His team had participants from all over the world. They kept their hacking attacks low key but built a massive offline system to control the interface with the Caligrian system.

In less than two weeks Matt was able to share the fact that they were able to listen to all conversation in the Caligrian control rooms on all four ships and they had gained access to the computer system.

Matt brought the lead linguistic specialist to a lunch meeting where he broke the news that a language translation program had been written that allowed English to be spoken and Caligrian to be transmitted.

Marshal took personal control of the ground battles.

He went to the field and got the soldiers and their field commanders to stop yielding ground. He coached them on how to disrupt and run. Then disrupt and run again.

He worked with the support centers to release everyone in the system for ground battle. The new troops hurried out to each of the battle areas.

More weapons and better shielding were sent to the field.

He arranged for the planes that had been hidden away to come back to the field and fly low level runs to disperse napalm.

Napalm cannons were quickly built and sent to the field.

The fifty-caliber machine gun made a battle comeback.

Marshal quickly got shrapnel dispersing land mines manufactured and deployed on all battlefield fronts.

The army was scheduled to fall back on the coordination attack date. They would fall back to lure the Caligrians into the area where new non-metallic land mines were positioned.

At the same time air support would swoop in with the napalm.

When the alien air support appeared the matter transmitter operators would target them.

The coordination of all these events was dispersed physically in a wide web of inter-connected individuals.

Out in the field, Marshal cried internally as he watched the bodies of the fallen carried off the battle fields. Then he ordered the field commanders to charge the line again.

Earth lost three soldiers for everyone Caligrian.

Marshal watched the charges, watched carnage, and then ordered the next charge.

Each time his field commanders cursed him, but they sent their troops in.

Emma took control of the information on the World-Wide Web. She made sure there was a constant stream of the dramatic losses by the Caligrians. The Caligrian fighters were shown running from battle, surrendering, or shown committing atrocities.

The casualties Earth was suffering was not communicated.

Emma was surprised that the lies being broadcast was having a positive effect on the world population. Volunteers to fight the Caligrians surged tenfold.

The ground battles became more fiercely contested. Captured shields were immediately put into use. Those on the battlefield began to have new confidence.

Once again, the Yellow Stone team came together at the base of Yuka mountain.

Marshal looked out at the others in the room.

He turned to those on the platform. Alton MacPherson was the one new addition to the team.

Marshal recognized his promotion and welcomed him to the team.

He thanked everyone at the table for their heroic effort.

Next, he walked off the platform, went to each table, and thanked each for the specific action they had personally taken.

The room was silent as he made his way to every person.

He returned to the platform and recognized those who he had been sent to battle and had sacrificed the most. He thanked them and promised to have their names remembered for eternity.

He had tears in his eyes as he signaled Emma to take over the meeting.

13 On the Verge of Victory

Vesian had objected to the battle with the inhabitants of the planet. On this first encounter with an intelligent race, they had broken their own guiding principal.

Maltar was breaking every rule designed to ensure peace in the universe. She and her supporters had argued against the current action Maltar had taken.

Maltar pointed out that Vesian's authority was only pertinent once the planet was colonized. Until then she should keep her advice to herself.

She had pushed to have a vote of confidence and to have the ships return to their home world.

Vesian had reminded everyone there were six additional worlds that did not have life on them.

Maltar countered with the fact that this system had no intelligent life on it when he had first visited.

The millions of years could have altered the other worlds as well.

His supporters chose to back Maltar.

Vesian held the same rank as Maltar and had a bigger following than he, but Maltar had control of the ships and of the weapons.

Vesian knew there was no way to physically intervene, but she set about aligning those who felt the Caligrian edict on not interfering with intelligent life was being broken. This Vesian knew would be important in resolving the final colonization arrangement.

She resolved that she would work at righting the wrong she felt was being committed.

Maltar walked the ship's military training deck. He regretted the day he had decided to focus on the commercial aspects and minimize the amount of small arms armament carried on the ships.

The fire power of the ships themselves was sufficient to annihilate the entire surface of the planet but that would defeat his desire to colonize a habitable planet.

The safety shielding became a major element of their ability to inflict damage while minimizing their casualties.

The Tans and Browns were providing adequate support to their Black commanders.

Maltar had conscripted all Blacks above the age of fifteen and placed them in leadership positions from platoon level on up. Now he wished he had selected an even higher percentage of Black colonists.

His transport ships had almost no weaponry. The mechanics had mounted lasers under the fuselage of the transports, and they were serving as formidable air support.

Maltar looked at the map of the battles and was pleased that soon the war would be over.

Earth was as good as his.

He would not be as charitable in dealing with these inferior species as he had been with his initial offer.

Maltar reviewed his intelligence report. It was clear the people of the planet had evolved to a very peaceful and stable situation.

They had no army, or weapons.

The planet did have twelve billion beings.

The report documented the fact that the Earthlings were turning out weapons in significant numbers with which to fight. Museum pieces were copied and were being mass produced in alarmingly large quantities.

He gave orders to his field commanders to accelerate their attacks and to push their adversaries into the kill formation.

He was pleased with the response to his orders. The battles were going as planned. His ships gave his army air superiority.

The Earth space vessels were hidden away to prevent their destruction. The air superiority allowed him to move his troops at will into strategic locations.

The Blacks who historically were the warrior class were novices. He was one of the few classically trained in the strategy of war and this was his first actual combat situation. The superior technology he possessed seemed to his fighters. They were a significant advantage.

His adversaries were fierce fighters but were not as well equipped as his army. Even though they outnumbered his army two to one he was slowly driving them back to the kill concentration points he had designated. The lasers on the transport ships would do the final annihilation and then he would dictate terms to the Earthlings as they called themselves.

The biggest issue was Vesian; she continued to object to the attacks on the planet. She had become a pain in his side but about half the Caligrians supported her. This made her dangerous and it made it difficult for Maltar to totally have his way.

Things were going exactly as he planned. He was sure of a victory in the very near future.

"Sir, we have picked up unusual dialogue and movement of troops. Their armies have stopped retreating they have dug in and are refusing to retreat. Reinforcements are coming at an unusually higher rate." one of his aides informed him.

"Tell the ground troops to press harder; they are on the verge of winning. They must push forward," Maltar replied to the information of the ground troop issues.

"By the way sir, Vesian has again called from her vessel. She continues to object to your continued war. This she says is counter to all teachings of our race," the aid continued.

"Inform her she will be able to send a formal complaint about me back to the homeland when the three transports return. Let her know she is welcome to return with them," Maltar replied.

He was about at the end of his patience in his dealing with Vesian. He would love to see her leave with the transports. He knew if she stayed, she would forever be working against him.

Maltar was surprised to learn that half of his original discovery crew was now on Vesian's side. The fact that such previously loyal friends would choose to stab him in the back after all he had done for them was incomprehensible to him.

He would deal with them when the battles came to an end. He would be generous to those who remained loyal. The rest would have to make their own way.

Maltar's orders went out. It seemed to work. The Earthlings all retreated.

The Caligrian armies followed.

Something had changed.

What had changed was invisible to the Caligrians, but the Earthlings retreat was minimal. The land mines disrupted the Caligrian frontline fighters. Then mortar fire started, simultaneously with heavy machine gun fire blended in.

When the first napalm cannons shot their charges and the flaming snakes hit the line of Caligrian fighters, they dropped their shields as in flames and agony they ran screaming from the battlefield.

Then low flying planes almost hugging the ground followed and dropped additional napalm.

The Caligrian forces were routed from the field and the Earthlings steadily retook the ground they had been grudgingly giving up.

Maltar listened but found it hard to comprehend.

Sir, our armies in all locations are retreating in mass.

A new unbelievable horrible weapon has been unleashed by the Earthlings.

Sir, the army is reporting huge casualties.

Several of our fighter craft reported being flooded with some sort of substance and have had to make emergency landings.

"Sir, the lights on the planet have extinguished," an aid spoke up.

Maltar looked at the screen at a totally black world. It was eerie.

What was going on?

He pounded on the control table in front of him and demanded to know what was going on.

He was on the verge of telling his ship captains to laser the battle fields when he started coughing. The air suddenly filled with a fine dust. His eyes were burning, and he was coughing violently as were all the other people in the control room.

"What is happening, he barked out.

"Sir all ships are being attacked with some matter that is making it through our shields. It is not fatal and seems to be a nutrient.

"Well, block its' flow whatever it is," Maltar said between coughs.

It was almost impossible to see across the room.

"Sir, if we block the incoming material, we will not be able to launch any additional support ships to the surface."

"Block it now and then we will figure how to get the support craft out," Maltar ordered.

As soon as the shields blocked the material, the next crisis surfaced.

The other transports are reporting the same air contamination and it's getting worse. They have followed our lead and blocked the inflow of material.

"What is happening with our transports," Maltar wanted to know

"They reported being overwhelmed with an inflow of material into the control rooms. They landed immediately or crashed."

"Sir we have lost the remainder of the transports assigned to provide the troops air support."

"Several have crashed among our troops, the rest landed and most have been overrun and taken over by the Earthlings."

"Sir, the Earthlings are advancing on our troops and have devised a way to overcome the shields.

"Sir, the field marshals are asking for your orders."

"Tell them to hold their ground. Send additional troops. We have another hundred transports. Put them all to use," Maltar barked his orders.

He tried to focus his burning eyes. It was hard to concentrate between the coughing and his burning eyes.

Sir, all the crafts are affected. They are experiencing the same situation we are. It is a struggle to just hold our position and the situation is getting worse.

"Block all incoming materials. The Earthlings have found some weakness in our shielding system. Let nothing through," Maltar ordered.

"Only open the shield long enough to let each ship through. Send the order out to each of the other vessels to do the same," Maltar barked out his orders.

If anything, the situation was getting worse. He was in a state of shock. How had this happened? They had been closely monitoring the earthling communications and had not gotten any indication of a change to their normal fighting approach.

"Sir, when we opened our shield to let the first ship out, it was immediately filled with material from the planet. The crew suffocated in their control room. We have closed the shield. The other transports have reported the same situation. We have four derelict ships floating toward the planet with almost four thousand troops."

Maltar was in a state of shock. How had the Earthlings been able to surprise him and his troops so completely?

The earthlings had been on the verge of defeat. He could use his laser cannons, but they would not be effective unless the Earthlings were tightly grouped.

"Sir, the Captains of the other transports are now siding with Vesian. Vesian has issued an order for the confrontation to cease. She is ready to concede this system to the Earthlings. She reminds you of the standing policy that we are not to encroach on other intelligences.

"Remind her, I command this expedition until we get the population on the ground," Maltar growled out as he cursed whatever the material the Earthlings had flooded the ship with.

"Sir, the earthlings have sent up their space craft and have boarded our four transports. They have taken them in tow and are guiding them down to their space ports.

"The troops on the ground have retreated and set up defensive positions. They are being asked to surrender or threatened with annihilation.

The field commanders ask your orders."

"Tell them to hold the line. The Earthlings can't just take over in an instant. They have sustained huge causalities. Tell our fighters to do what they have been doing so effectively," Maltar shouted back.

He was almost being driven crazy by the condition on the ship and the inept behavior of his field commanders.

Suddenly the room went dark.

"Abandon the control room and retreat to the emergency control room," Maltar shouted as the dust began to overwhelm him.

"Sir, the Earthlings have penetrated our shield. They concentrated everything they had on a focused shield point and penetrated to the generator. All our shields are down, and we are totally exposed. We are rapidly being filed with earth soil.

The other three transports are untouched. This control room and our ship is the focal point.

The emergency power came on and the room glowed amber. The air was noticeably thicker with dust. Suddenly the soil began to pour into the control room. If it did not stop soon, they would all suffocate.

"Sir, we can't get the doors open,"

"Sir, we are getting communication coming in from the Earthlings. They are speaking to us in our language."

This pushed Maltar over the edge. This was impossible. How had the Earthlings made such a turn around? They had been losing the fight on a two to one basis.

How had they learned the Caligrian language so quickly?

"This surrender request is addressed to Maltar.

We do not desire to annihilate you and your fighters, but we will do what we must to defend our world.

We will continue to give you the earth you requested but it will suffocate you and your people in the ships you came on. We have demonstrated our ability to penetrate your defenses.

Your troops on the ground will surrender in the next hour or we will attack with the goal of total destruction. We will use the weapons on your own ships to carry out this threat.

If you have studied our past, you know we were vicious fighters and have used horrible weapons against each other. We have reconstituted one of the most horrifying weapons called napalm. We used this sparingly to route your troops. Please review the pictures we are sending so you understand the horrible nature of this weapon. This will be dropped on all your troops when the hour is up. Next, we will beam this material into the transport ships. We await your response. Please continue to monitor our net. You will learn many things you thought we did not know."

"Sir, Vesian is on the com for you.

"Maltar, it is time you stepped back from the brink of self-destruction. We were all sent the same communication. My people have done a quick search of the weapon they speak of. It is a liquid combustible gel that sticks to you and burns. It is an unbelievably horrible weapon.

We do not have anything like that in our history. Our soldiers in the field who have been hit by this are suffering greatly. Their second weapon they did not speak of was the landmine. When stepped on the mine explodes and maims you. These beings should be left alone. You have made a terrible choice in this situation. You have awakened a demon and have put all of our people at risk," Vesian said with emotion.

"Sir, all attacks have stopped. We are monitoring the Earth communication network.

They are showing our home star and planet and accompanying it with the message, *"Let us tell you about the mathematics of your time folding technique. We have it as well. We now know where you came from"* and then they are showing our dead soldiers with the caption, *"and this is how we will send you back. A billion if we must. If necessary, we will finish the job on location at your home world."*

Maltar sat in stunned silence. His mind was running in circles trying to find a door. His eyes were watering, and he went from one coughing fit to another.

The control room was silent except for the coughing of all individuals.

A short time later Vesian took over command of the four vessels.

Maltar remained incoherent and had to be restrained in the medical ward. He had lost control of his mind. He was taken to babbling and screaming orders incoherently into the restraining room.

Vesian immediately sent her capitulation message.

"To the people of Earth, let me extend my apology. We will cease our attacks. We surrender. May we recover our fighters?" Vesian sent the message out a few minutes before the deadline.

Emma made the reply for Earth.

Three of your ships will depart back to your home planet immediately.

The people on the fourth ship will be welcomed on Mars and a few will be hosted on Earth.

This fourth craft will be confiscated and become part of Earth's defense.

You have many wounded personnel on the surface. We are doing all we can for them but please send your doctors.

Vesian was surprised at the demand. She had not thought about this possibility. She consulted with the captains of the four transports.

The captain of Maltar's transport volunteered to stay with his ship.

It seemed the Earthlings were being fair considering the threat they had faced. It also seemed they had somehow learned some key information about the Caligrians and their technology.

"We are not in a very good position to bargain, but I must make sure I do not leave my people here to become enslaved. I would much rather run with the ships and people I have than let that happen," Vesian sent out the inquiry.

The reply; *"Be assured we have evolved to be generous and sharing. We did not initiate the battle. We tried multiple times to end the situation. We are not interested in treating anyone unjustly.*

Vesian addressed all the people on the four transports.

"This is a sad time for all of us. We departed our beloved Caligria with hopes of making our home on a lush world in this system. A terrible mistake was made when we did not follow our own principle of not interfering with the worlds having intelligent life.

After some consideration, I have elected to stay. The Earthling's insist Maltar stays and faces trial in Earth's legal system.

I am to attend a planning session with the Earthlings in their global capital of New York. The membership of the fourth and remaining transport will be made up of volunteers wishing to stay. It seems the Earthlings only prosecute the leaders and not the fighters so all but Maltar and several field commanders are free to do as they please.

This is different than Caligrian history. We would punish everyone. The three captains of the transport ships will return to Caligria with all other immigrants. Perhaps once we spend more time with the Earthlings, we will be able to bring more settlers into this solar system. I wish all the best for your lives and may we meet again in the near future," Vesian finished her somber address.

Marshal had sent a contingent of Earth's military as a symbol of the capitulation of the Caligrians.

They used the storage chambers to set up the Earth command center. This area was large enough to house them without modifying the structure of the Transport.

The Earthling's were polite but firm. They were studying all the technology on board. They especially were focusing on the power generators used to generate the power for the time-space fold drive. The drive itself was being studied by the woman emissary, Emma sent up to work with Vesian.

The Caligrian soldiers in the field were treated and sent up to their transport ships. The downed alien air support craft were all confiscated. These went immediately into reverse engineering facilities. The four scout ships possessing the fold capability were confiscated along with the fourth transport ship.

The fold transmitters were immediately copied.

Vesian was surprised at the relatively gentle treatment the leaders of Earth extended to the Caligrians.

She met with Marshal and the rest of the team she understood to have guided the turnaround of the battle between them.

Marshal seemed very levelheaded and calm. She was surprised he was the one who had recalled and let loose such vile weapons.

14 Into the Future

arshal savored the victory but knew that the recovery from the ravages of the battle would take years to repair.

Most of the Caligrians were settling on Mars. There were multiple generations of transformation work to make Mars into a comfortable habitat.

He knew that it was time for him to move on. He was the extraction accident.

He asked both Matt and Andrew if they were OK with staying in Emma's time.

He knew Matt and Samantha were perfectly happy and seemed to have acclimated to the current culture.

Andrew had found someone that seemed to make him happy.

He was not surprised when Matt said he and Samantha were planning their wedding. They had not even thought about going back to their own time. They were home.

Andrew added that he had suggested a double wedding and that he and Anton would certainly be staying in this current time.

Andrew also pointed out that in their original time they were to have an accident and die. If they went back and lived, he wondered how that would affect the timeline.

Marshal was sure that in every case the historic timeline would be affected. He was not going to worry about it. He had the feeling that the future had manipulated the timeline multiple times.

He mentioned to Matt and Andrew the fact that they had come from their time to this time and had remained awake and conscious. This was either due to the improved genes Emma had been sending back or some future Emma had sent back.

For all you know the future beyond Emma's current time arranged for your accident so that Emma would extract you to this time.

My job was to pass on my DNA to you two not to get extracted with Samantha.

Andrew, you suggested we go to the future to find out what we needed to know to beat the Caligrians. We did not go because the near future is blocked.

He let the four know that he had worked with Cardasian Lieberman, a top-notch technician in the Extraction and Reinsertion area to set up a jump into the far future. Cardasian had verified that the near future was blocked but that future some twenty thousand years out was open.

He let them know he was going to take the leap forward.

"So, what has this to do with the question about us all going back to our own time," Andrew asked in what appeared to be an irritated tone.

"Well, by going into the future, I will learn if we would cause any disturbance in the time space continuum or whatever you want to call the history of the people of the world." Marshal replied.

"Ok, but why so far into the future. If you fall through that much time you may end up being nothing but a splatter mark on the floor," Matt suggested.

Marshal replied that he had confidence that the future would perfect the science and the technical aspects of extraction and reinsertion.

He stated his confidence that the future would catch him and be able to send him back to this specific time.

Andrew asked when he was planning to make the jump.

Marshal smiled and replied that it was planned after lunch time.

He was not allowing for debate and he was by-passing all the official channels.

He already knew Emma would balk.

She was currently busy with the resettling of the Caligrians and was not involved in much of the time travel work.

He had unofficially taken over guiding the extraction effort simply by asking questions of those working for her. She had left word to support him and that was enough to free and feed his curiosity.

"OK, what would you like us to do?" Matt asked.

"Well, if I am wrong you can clean up the mess. Most likely you will just be watching me wink out and then wink back in. I will ask those in the future to be as precise as they are able and return me to as close the time I left as possible. I will however ask to be brought back at least ten minutes into your future. This will give you a measure to ensure I really made the trip," Marshal continued.

Marshal replied that if he were wrong, Matt and Andrew would need to mollify Emma. If I am right, I will return ten minutes after I leave. The ten minutes are only so you will know that I actually took the trip and it worked out as planned.

After lunch, Marshal led the way into the extraction-reinsertion room.

Cardasian was animated in his excitement. He dutifully set the reinsertion for twenty thousand years into the future. He asked if Marshal was confident that this insertion into the future was going to work.

Marshal chuckled and said that he was not sure he was all that confident. He was apprehensive. He could be totally wrong about the far future. He might end up, unable to return.

This made him stop and hug Matt, Andrew, and Samantha. That was just in case I am wrong.

I am proud of all of you.

He stepped into the focal point of the time vortex and signaled Cardasian to activate.

The fall seemed to go on for a long time.

Marshal was trying to keep track but lost count multiple times. He thought he might have counted to ten thousand but was no longer sure.

The darkness was complete.

He was totally disoriented as to the direction of his fall. It reminded him of the time when he had been surfing off Oahu's North shore and been sucked under. He struggled to figure out which way up was. He almost drowned but when he hit the bottom he got reoriented and came up coughing and sputtering.

He hoped for more than a splatter on his arrival in the future.

Then he saw the light.

"Welcome to the future, Marshal. We have been waiting for you. You are our one anomaly that made time travel work," a rather refined looking human spoke in perfect English.

Marshal thanked the person for bringing him in so gently and stood perfectly still as she scanned him with a magicians wand.

"Yes, it was a few years after your experience when the ability to sense incoming travelers was developed. Shortly after that the ability to land them softly was added.

The Samuels landing mat is still studied as the starting point," the human who Marshal decided was a woman informed him.

"I am known as Marial. I am one of a billion humans who still remain in physical form. There are many billions more living in the Net. Let me be your guide for a short period of time. Be assured you will be able to do as you wish with no negative consequences.

Please follow me and I will show you your living quarters.

We brought you in onto one of our geocentric orbiting cities.

You will see that Earth has become a wondrous place to visit on vacations and family outings. It is almost un-populated. The only people who actually reside there most of the time are those engaged in the upkeep and continuing naturalization of the planet," Marial said as she introduced herself.

"For her time Emma certainly did a good job on rejuvenating you." We will trim and tune you up before sending you back to maximize your existence.

There is a finite period for our bodies but as you will learn during your stay, we are now able to transfer ourselves into the net. Periodically we can utilize a physical body when we need to act more physically.

"Well, I have a very practical reason for making this leap into the future. I would like to return to my original time period and be with my wife for the remainder of the years we can share.

I need to know that there will be no negative impact as to the space-time-history sequence continuum," he came right to the point.

He had decided to get right to the point of his travel into the far future. He wanted to return to his original time and be with his wife when she learned that Matt and Andrew were missing.

He wanted to spend the remainder of his time with her. He wanted to know this was possible and posed no risk to the space, time, an history sequence continuum.

And separately he asked about the relationship between the Caligrians and Earth.

Marial replied to his last question first.

"Earth and the Caligrians are close partners in the exploration of space. So far, we are the only two intelligent species that have discovered each other. The Caligrians are spread across six solar systems and Earthlings are spread across another three solar systems. Our populations are about equal.

The occurrence of the two species finding one another was a miracle in the estimation of all those who have continued the search for other intelligence. The Caligrian population in Earth's solar system remained at the level first established at the end of the immigration battle." Marial informed Marshal.

"Is the human race evolving to a higher level of intelligence," he asked?

"No, it is interesting you should ask because we have been wondering if we ourselves stopped the process of evolution.

It seems all the points in time when the human or any other species evolved was during a period of stress or threat to the continued existence of the species.

We of course have developed amazing technologies and made significant advances in all fields. But the basic intelligence of the human has not changed since your time. One theory was that the physical nature of our brains reached the optimum at about your time.

If we turned you loose on your own, you would be lost in dealing with today's technology but that is a matter of learning not of basic intelligence. You would soon learn all of our technology.

In fact, one of our advances is how new knowledge is learned. We are able to inject knowledge into the brain and have it create new neural connections by directing the messages to the brain. This means we may not be smarter, but we have much more information available in our brains," Marial responded.

He continued his inquiry.

Emma was trying to send people back in time to accelerate the human development. I came to the conclusion that I and my sons were the result of some later successes in doing just that. The acceleration of human development did indeed occur so we could match the capabilities of the Caligrians.

I was indeed an accident of the moment, but my sons were the intended retrieval of accelerated human development.

Do I have this about right?"

"Yes, actually it was Emma that did successfully send people back, but it was so because she learned from you what to do. This in turn resulted in you and your sons.

It only worked because you were never on record as having made the journey forward in time. I am not sure I understand my own explanation or how this timeline can be explained." Marial replied.

He thanked Marial. He knew now what he had to do on his return to Emma's time.

He then asked about his sons and Emma.

"I cannot tell you because we are concerned about the impact on the timeline. Let me just say all is well," was Marial's polite reply.

"We have planned two major tours for you while you are here," Marial went on, "One is a tour to Mars where the Caligrians want to honor you and then on your return there will be a tour of the cities of Earth.

He was a surprised about the situation, but he went on the tour.

He visited Mars.

What a thrill it was to travel from the city to Mars through the time-space portal. The transfer was almost immediate.

Once there he was greeted by the Caligrians in a parade and a dinner in his honor.

He was surprised to see a statue of himself with Emma, Andrew, Matt, and Samantha.

The inscription on the statue was, "The four who taught the Caligrians the meaning of adherence to Principles."

Marshal was baffled by the inscription and asked what it meant.

"The story goes that the four of you made a point of the fact the Caligrians broke their own principle of not disturbing another civilization. You made Maltar and Vesian, the leaders who had broken this rule, stay and live on Mars to teach them a lesson of principle.

It seems Maltar never recovered from his defeat and Vesian went on to redeem herself as the leader of the first Caligrian settlers," Marial recited the story of the statue.

"Well, I am honored to have a statue of the four of us. But Vesian should have the credit for how the Caligrians became friends with Earth. It turns out she and more than half of the Caligrians did not want to encroach on the Earth's solar system when they discovered intelligent life. They were ready to leave immediately.

However, Maltar had the belief he had the superior technology and the dire need because of the dying star in his home system. This was enough for him to decide to encroach. He began by offering the people of Earth a share of their own solar system.

You know the rest.

However, we wanted Maltar to stay because we wanted to keep close tabs on him.

Does the saying, "Keep your friends close and your enemies' closer?" still exist. We decided Maltar needed to be kept very close so he would never have the opportunity to break that principle again.

Vesian on the other hand began immediately to heal the wounds on both sides. She is truly a person of honor. You should add her to the statue with her hand extended in friendship," he shared with the group he was sitting with for dinner.

"This evening you have lived up to the reputation you earned from the Caligrians," Marial told him on their way back to the transport center.

"What do you mean?" he asked puzzled by her comment.

"You have been described as a person, hard as steel, one that could be brutal when confronted by unjust action and very generous in all other actions," Marial responded.

"I would put it in more practical terms. *I am only human*," he said with a chuckle.

After similar parades and dinners in his honor back on Earth and several months of general learning and satisfying his curiosity, he approached Marial.

He had soaked up the knowledge of the spread of the Human and Caligrian expansion through the Universe.

He was a little overwhelmed by the many myths that had sprung up about him and the battles against the Caligrians.

He knew it was time to return to Emma's time period to complete a few specific tasks and then to return to the time of his origin.

He asked Marial if she would be able to return him to his time prior to his accidental extraction by Emma. He shared his speculation that he had never been reported as missing because Marial would send him back and he would be there with his wife and daughter when Matt and Andrew went missing.

He had his writing for many years after that.

Marial confirmed that she would be able to send him back close to that time period.

I will arrange for you to return to Emma's time a few moments after your departure. You will need to come back here and we will then send you back to your own original starting time.

"Before your return I have one surprise for you. Vesian is still with us as is Emma.

Vesian has excited the World-Wide and downloaded into a current body. She would like to have dinner with you. She heard of your support for her and was touched. She recalls many hard but fair negotiations with you. Your support for correcting her place in history reinforces her initial assessment of your character.

Emma, Samantha, your sons and all the people you know in Emma's time frame are also in the web. They are aware of your visit and have followed you very closely.

However, they will not be allowed to meet you directly because it may cause an unknown loop in the time continuum. Vesian will bring you all their thoughts and good wishes." Marial gave Marshal the news.

He thanked her and said he was really excited to have dinner with Vesian. He was sure he would learn some critical information. He was a little overwhelmed by this last piece of information.

Andrew had called it. In his birth time, Andrew had predicted that one day the human entity would become a virtual being. Humans would not evolve they would morph into virtual beings.

There were tears of joy in his eyes. The peace this brought him could not be measured.

"Perhaps sometime in the future, you can arrange for my return visit to this time." Marshal said to Vesian and Marial after dinner as they walked toward the transport area.

"You will live into the time period where we can reach you and we will, but that cycle has not yet happened as we talk today. After you leave the second time we will know when you return. These timelines are still confusing even after all the work we do in trying to understand them," Marial said with a smile.

15 Caligria

Marshal blinked out of Marial's presence. He felt a smooth acceleration and then amazingly he blinked into existence. The far future had significantly improved the folding of time and space and the movement of people within it.

"Well, this is about as much warning as he ever gives when he is about to do something others would argue with," Matt said to no one in particular.

"What's going on here?" Emma said as she came rushing in.

She was out of breath and upset that she had not been informed. She had learned through her grapevine that Marshal was playing with time travel to the future.

"Well, in ten minutes or so you will be able to ask the culprit of your concern directly. Until that time we are not totally sure ourselves of what is going on." Andrew replied

"What happens in ten minutes?" Emma asked.

"Marshal plans to return from the future," Samantha took her turn replying to Emma.

"The future, we have tried before and have not been able to send anyone forward. Why does he think he can do it?" Emma pointed her question at Cardasian

Marshal chose twenty thousand years into the future," was Cardasian's quiet answer.

"Twenty thousand years, why so far when we know landing is such an issue?" Emma said worriedly to no one in particular.

"Well, we do know that reason. Marshal felt they would have solved the landing problem by then. He also felt with the new knowledge you will get from the arrival of the Caligrians you will be able to solve the arrival problems in the near future. He is counting on your future success to keep him from splatting into the ground in that future. How is that for believing in your friends?" Samantha said with a smile on her face.

"How much longer do I have to wait before I ask him myself?" Emma asked.

"We have a couple of minutes left," Matt replied.

In his mind and memory Marshal had been gone almost a year. He mentally knew he was coming back only ten minutes later then when he had departed. It was a struggle to remember he had left Matt, Samantha and Andrew standing with bewildered looks on their faces.

He blinked out from the transport room where Marial and Vesian had just given him hugs and to him he almost immediately blinked into the receiving area where Matt, Samantha, Andrew, and a stern looking Emma stood looking at him.

The transport back seemed almost instantaneous.

It took him a few seconds to respond.

"They certainly had perfected the process in the future," he had time to think before he embraced an on-rushing Emma.

"What in the world made you think you would survive this experiment," Emma asked as she stepped back from Marshal.

"I knew you would ensure my success," Marshal answered with a smile, "Did you notice my return; fully clothed, on my feet, no icicles?"

"How long were you gone in your mind?" Emma asked.

"I was gone almost a year. They said you did a very good job at rejuvenating me but tuned me up while I was there. I came back to say goodbye but also to ensure history is properly recorded.

Much of the detail of our meeting with the Caligrians has gotten confused. We need to ensure more clarity as to the final resolution and to put it clearly on the World-Wide.

"What is it like twenty thousand years in the future?

Do we evolve to be thin sticks with big heads?

Are we replaced with a more advanced model?"

Matt asked with curiosity clearly evident.

"I will tell you all is well in the future and your efforts in the near future are critical in ensuring that well-being. I cannot tell you more without risking the future. Those in the future still have not figured out the impact of certain detailed knowledge going back in time.

I am the one person who somehow got randomly out of control by shear chance. The future is willing to humor me because I seem to be an agent of good change and they have no consistent and clear history for me but wait for it to periodically show up. Even in their time they are still debating the impact of knowledge going back in time.

They are less afraid of the evolutionary change of speeding the knowledge build and the DNA repair work Emma is doing because they recognize the change does not have a large physical impact." Marshal replied.

Andrew interpreted for the room the Marshal had just declared that people in the far future were still pretty much the same as their current form.

"So, what is next?" Andrew asked.

"Will Mom be there in the future?" Matt asked, though he thought he already knew the answer.

"No, not yet" was all Marshal was willing to say.

He had come up with a plan to change that, but he was not sure how it would work or whether he would be able to change that part of the timeline.

This was a point about time travel the future still did not know how to deal with. The ability to transfer a person's mental being into the World-Wide directly was a point that had not been totally examined. From Emma's time forward the minds of all individuals were recorded in the World-Wide.

Their bodies died but their being was held as a digital construct in the World Wide Web. The past before Emma's time could be retrieved but the live body needed to make the trip.

To retrieve all the people of the past would mean having to pull everybody from the past. This would leave the past with missing bodies that no longer took the actions affecting history. What would the future be if the bodies removed were critical for the course of history?

The debate in the far future was whether the past being should be pulled forward just as they died. How to do this without affecting history was still an issue. Bodies were processed when they died. If every dying person's body were brought forward just a moment before death how would the past deal with this mystery?

How would it change the future?

He listed the three things he wanted to accomplish before he departed.

He identified a trip to the Caligrian System to establish the foundation of mutual cooperation and friendship.

He pointed to getting the events to the Earth-Caligrian relationship establishment properly recorded.

Another action was the improvement of Emma's reinsertion technique so they could all become who they were.

Andrew immediately understood.

"So, unless we improve the re-insertion technique, we may never exist and then we could not make this improvement so that we can come into existence. It seems like the dog chasing his tail," Andrew said.

"How about having dinner at the lodge tonight?" Marshal said leading the way out of the time vortex room.

Emma, please ask Vesian to join us.

Marshal went into detail of his plans to visit Caligria.

Vesian was surprised at his proposal but she listened politely.

Marshal suggested that the colonization transport ship be loaned back to the Caligrians to accelerate their colonization of other worlds. The ship would be staffed by a crew from Earth.

He pointed out that this would be mutually beneficial to both races. Earth would gain tremendous knowledge.

Emma concurred with the loan of the transport ship but pointed out the likely resistance they would get from the leaders of Earth.

Marshal agreed that there needed to be a significant gain for Earth to get worldwide support.

He suggested the loan include the requirement that the Caligrians train several thousand scientists and engineers in the Caligrian sciences. He pointed out this would leapfrog Earth's knowledge and put them on equal footing with the Caligrians.

"I think I can convince the Caligrians," Vesian finally spoke.

She was now seeing Marshal with new eyes. He really was truly looking for the best for all involved.

Emma said she would contact the President. If they got his support the rest of the world would follow.

She was excited about this partnership with the Caligrians.

She suspected Marshal was acting on knowing something about the future. Either that it had been done or it should have been done.

Marshal had always been unpredictable but now Emma knew she would only be guessing about his motives.

"I would love to be among the first to spend time learning the Caligrian sciences," Matt said as the discussion hit a lull.

Alton and I both would love to as well Andrew added.

Marshal asked Vesian to make the plans and the arrangements for their travel.

He suggested they send an unmanned communication module through to the Caligrian system announcing the near future visit from Earth.

Once again Vesian was surprised. For the first time since the surrender, she felt true hope for their mutual races.

Marshal walked behind the group with Samantha and asked her to accept the responsibility to work with the sculptor of a statue that was currently being designed.

Samantha looked at the sketch he handed her and replied that she would make sure to get the sculptor to reproduce the sketch. She could not resist a little tease and added that she hoped the sculptor was better at sculpting than he was at sketching.

Marshal and Vesian stood behind the navigator of the scout ship. Vesian had selected the Captain of the transport ship to be the navigator. She and the Captain were the only two Caligrians returning.

The scout ship was loaded with communication cubes from the Caligrian colonists to friends and family.

Matt commented that a regular mail system should be established.

Vesian looked at Marshal and got an approving nod.

The transition through the space time fold went without incident.

He and the team stood transfixed by the black silhouette of the Caligrian planet against the giant red star that was the equivalent of the Earth's sun. The dominance of the star displaced all other aspects of the Caligrian solar system

Vesian shared that an inner planet had already been consumed by the stars dying expansion. Of the seven remaining planets only Caligria and the next planet out was habitable.

He commented that the sight of the huge red star put fear in his heart for the people of Caligria and he now better understood Maltar's actions.

The captain pointed out that they were being hailed by one of a dozen ships as they emerged from the fold.

Both Marshal and Vesian were surprised but their friendly greeting put them at ease.

The ships were an honor guard sent out to greet and to escort them to the landing site.

Marshal was the first out of the hatch and smiled when he saw the red carpet being rolled up to the bottom of the ramp. That two totally different intelligences, on worlds billions of miles apart would have so similar a formal greeting ceremony spoke of the miracle of divine intervention.

Look team, a red carpet greeting.

"Who would have thought," Andrew said quietly.

Marshal walked down the ramp, with Vesian on one side and Emma on the other. The rest of the team followed closely behind.

Vesian made a point of introducing each of the dignitaries either by name and when she did not know their name, she indicated rank and let the dignitary introduce themselves.

In a surprise to the dignitaries and Vesian, he and Emma greeted the dignitaries in the Caligrian language.

Vesian later shared that the two had accelerated the bonding of the two races by hundreds of years.

The team was escorted to a large meeting hall. Marshal likened it to a large convention dining room. He and the team were seated at a table placed up on a platform in the middle of the room.

He stopped counting tables when he reached one hundred. Each table had a black center piece. The chairs around each table were similar to any earth table chair but was a little narrower and had longer legs.

He immediately felt the difference as he sat down. His butt spilled over the edges and his feet dangled just above the floor.

Emma laughed and commented that she had gained weight on coming through the fold.

Matt looking like an adult sitting in a kids chair stoically asked what she meant.

Vesian, who had been pulled to the side, returned to inform them that their dinner would be sent out from the scout ship.

The dinner would be accompanied with some speeches. Vesian shared that there was an expectation that he, and Emma would reciprocate.

Emma immediately responded that Marshal should represent the team. She led the team in listing the key points of what to say.

He listened but did not take any notes.

After one Caligrian speaker, identified as the Supreme Caligrian Commander, similar to a world president finished his speech, Vesian stood, made a few opening remarks, and introduced Marshal.

He spoke slowly but clearly in Caligrian.

He took the time to introduce and explain the role of each of the Earth team members.

He elevated Vesian to the status of a Caligrian ambassador to Earth.

This was the first of multiple times he had to stop his speech as the audience either slapped the table or stomped their feet or both.

His message was one of friendship and working together. He emphasized the miracle of the two intelligent civilizations discovering each other and the partnership they would have into the distant future.

He shared his amazement and fear of seeing their red star and the need to ensure the Caligrians were safely migrated to other habitable worlds. He then offered the use of the confiscated transport to help get the Caligrians to these other worlds.

At this point, he had to pause as a standing ovation of table thumping and foot stomping Caligrians made speaking impossible.

He suggested an exchange program as a means to accelerate the two worlds learning about each other and received heavy applause.

When he announced a communication exchange utilizing information cubes to keep the Caligrians connected with each other no matter what world they were on. He was again stopped by table slapping.

He turned the floor back to Ambassador Vesian.

Vesian waited a few moments and then thanked the leaders for giving them the honor of the dinner.

Marshal encouraged the team to negotiate aggressively on getting what they wanted. He also wanted to make sure the Caligrians were pulled into getting grounded in Earth culture.

He reviewed the agreements and insisted on an equal number of exchange students from each race were engaged in learning about the other culture.

He made it clear the use of the transport was a loan and it would be staffed by an Earth crew.

He was getting use to manipulating his movement in time.

The team spent almost three months in Caligria but returned to Earth three days after their departure.

This time precision was the result of Emma and her team finally understanding the space time fold relationship in a more detailed way.

Emma admitted that she had planned the return for a full seven days after their initial departure and that additional tuning was required.

He praised Emma on the breakthrough. He knew that Emma would continue to improve the technique to the point the future would be able to control it to the hundredth of a second.

16 Distant Past

*T*heir return from Caligria made the Worldwide News and there were a few celebrations that included the team.

Vesian was formally recognized by the World Council leaders as an official Ambassador from Caligria.

And the Statue that Samantha had worked on with the sculptor was unveiled on Mars.

He the sculptor for the good work and pointed to the fact that he really had made everyone look better than in his original sketch.

He had one more task on his to do list before returning to his own time. He had come to realize that Emma would have two successful re-insertions.

The first had already occurred. He knew that story by heart as did ninety percent of the people of his time.

It was the story of Adam and Eve.

Emma admitted to more than a dozen re-insertions.

The second successful re-insertion would be the one that resulted in he, Matt, and Andrew being available for extraction. And because of the unknown in the far future, he had visited, he knew that Emma's next re-insertion had not yet happened.

He had some ideas on how to make the next re-insertion a success and he was going to guide the team in developing this reinsertion technology.

Marshal recalled the experience of his first extraction. He envisioned the situation when he had finally caught up with Samantha and they had both fallen into the extraction tunnel. He realized that both he and Samantha were sweaty from the exertion of jogging up the hill.

It made sense to him that water might be the key to ensuring a successful re-insertion.

Marshal called the team together to share his thoughts about encapsulating the next re-insertion in ice as a means to protect them.

Matt pointed out that the person being reinserted would be unconscious.

Samantha added that the impact might still kill the person being reinserted.

"Why not create an ice container within a container with slush acting as a hydraulic cushion. This would all melt and free the participant un-harmed.

The person would be in a bubble filled with oxygen rich slush. It would be an oxygen rich liquid like the ultra-deep sea divers use," Andrew volunteered as the concept took shape in his mind.

Marshal looked at the team and asked if they agreed to let Andrew guide the project he had just described.

The person being sent back was Marshal's next focus. He looked at Emma and asked what shot she had given to Samantha upon her extraction.

Emma explained that it was a nutrient to boost the survival response of the body. Early arrivals seemed to be in an anemic state. This is followed with relaxants to prevent shock

Marshal proposed a slow-release nutrient booster be put into the stomach. And rather than a relaxant, the person should immediately be given a shot of adrenaline to ensure the person was awake and had the capability to defend themselves.

Samantha volunteered to work with Emma on getting the person prepared to be awakened on arrival.

Matt, Andrew, and Alton spent the next month designing and testing prototypes of reinsertion vessels. Since their prototypes were made from water, the development and prototype costs were low.

Finally, they were ready to demonstrate the most successful prototype to the rest of the team.

Marshal walked around what to him looked like a giant icicle. He listened as Matt explained that the bottom half was solid ice to ensure the vessel would fall into the ground vertically.

The top third was the cushioning chamber that had an interior ice oxygen rich slush chamber where the person being re-inserted would be.

They had successfully tested the current version three times.

Andrew announced that the next test would include a volunteer female who would simulate the reinsertion situation.

Matt pointed out that it was his design, and he should be the guinea pig. The team had decided on a volunteer that most closely matched the height and weight of the three upcoming reinsertions.

Samantha described how the last three tests had utilized crash test dummies to understand the forces exerted on the human body. The consistency and viscosity of the suspension slush was adjusted to ensure an optimum landing force.

She and Emma had worked with the current volunteer and simulated the drug release effect and timing. This allowed them to adjust the dosage of the nutrients and how to administer the adrenalin booster.

Emma devised an ice syringe that on impact would shoot the adrenalin into the arm muscle.

The nutrients would be frozen in ice and be in the stomach.

Marshal was introduced to the volunteer and asked her if she were confident about the outcome of the upcoming simulation.

He jokingly asked Samantha and Emma how much they had paid to get such praise from the volunteer.

The test capsule was brought out of the "freezer" as they had dubbed the building holding the twenty-foot icicle looking capsule. The volunteer was lowered into the oxygen enriched slush. She was conscious and squinted her eyes as she slowly breathed in the oxygen rich slush.

Emma had already inserted the nutrient slush ball into the volunteer's stomach. She now pushed the ice syringe in the shoulder muscle.

Marshal wondered if he could have done what this volunteer was doing.

The capsule was sealed.

Matt was in charge of the controlled drop from a three-hundred-foot height.

Waiting for the ice to melt was the worst part of the test. The young lady inside was being monitored closely. Her vital signs stayed steady and she slowly revived. The ice capsule melted as designed and she swooshed out the bottom in a pile of slush and water.

The jolt and the drugs brought her fully awake.

Her first action had to be defensive.

Matt had arranged for a trained dog to attack her.

The volunteer reaction was to pick up a near-by stick and defend herself.

This was her first experience at being attacked. Her response was swift, and the dog had to be rescued.

Marshal had wanted to learn if the waking woman would have the ability to immediately defend herself. The response was swift and true.

The dog was rescued just in time.

He declared the test a success.

The debriefing revealed the test subject was not aware of any of the events until the dog was attacking. Her instincts took over and she grabbed the nearest object to defend herself.

She was a dog lover and was shocked at her aggressive response.

Marshal thanked the volunteer for ensuring the success of the next reinsertion.

He was certain the world where the three women would be reinserted would be very wild and they would most likely face even greater dangers. They would face wolves or perhaps lions.

An aggressive awakening might cause a few animals their deaths, but it would allow the women to survive.

Marshal asked what knowledge programing was being given to the women to be reinserted.

Emma listed survival skill, how to make fire, how to make a clay oven, how to prepare and cook various game and birds, how to build a shelter and how to make clothes from leather and the identification of a host of plants and basic first aid.

She made the point that the women would be a valuable asset to the community in which they end up.

Marshal asked whether they were getting any language skill or about the customs of the time?

Samantha asked what language he had in mind.

Marshal let his ideas roll out. They should have basic sign language and drawing skills. They should also be made sensitive to the protocol of the people they encounter. Men may be dominant, and they may need to act subservient, but they need to be able to take control if necessary. They need to be quick reads on this situation.

"There is one more thing that is important. They will awaken totally nude. They need a big dose of self-confidence. Is there a way to imprint martial art knowledge and the actual movements into their minds?" Marshal asked.

"Yes, we can do this but for them to be proficient they will have to practice. Their memory imprints would allow them to be black belt level in very short order," Emma replied.

"Well, let's do it and put an urge for them to practice. I want them to be the warrior amazons of ancient lore," he shared his thoughts.

Next he asked about the reinsertion strategy.

"We have decided to send all three women back to the same time period and if we are lucky, they will land next to each other," Emma answered.

Andrew suggested they send all three back in one reinsertion capsule.

The room went silent.

He looked at Andrew and smiled and commented about such a simple and elegant solution.

Matt chuckled and made a brotherly comment about even a broken clock was right twice a day. Then asked why he hadn't proposed this earlier.

Samantha gave Matt a gentle slap on the back of his head. Be nice she said quietly.

Emma was immediately excited. She acknowledged the need for additional power, but she would be able to get all she needed from one of the Caligrian shuttles.

Andrew pointed out the contradiction in the timeline. He wondered how they could be using Caligrian technology to send back DNA to enhance the human to be able to defeat the Caligrians.

Marshal agreed that there appeared to be a contradiction. However, Emma's program had never been set up to counter the Caligrians.

So, let's get on with the reinsertion of all three at one time.

The team focused on creating a three-person version of their reinsertion icicle.

A month later the three women who Marshall knew would go onto become the Amazon Warrior legends were launched into the distant past.

17 Return to the Origin

arshal was finally ready to go home to his time. He prepared to make the trip back to the future so he could be returned to his original time in the past.

He knew his hardest task was to say goodbye to his sons. In his mind he knew he would catch up to all that his sons would do and accomplish but, in his heart, he also knew he would live for years wondering each day how they were faring.

That they were together and had their mates was very comforting. He hoped he could somehow convey this to his wife. As he thought about this dilemma an idea came to him.

He would need a favor from the far future for him to convince someone in the distant past.

Matt voiced the feeling of everyone that they hated to see him leave and that they all wished him well.

Andrew said how comforting it was to know that Marshal would be there to comfort their mother.

And the next time that we meet we will be able to talk about all the things you knew we would go on to do. Hopefully, they will be pleasant discussions about our great accomplishments.

"Here, I thought I was the mature older person and found out I had so much to learn from such a young man. I have grown to love you," Emma whispered during her hug.

"I feel the same about you." Marshal whispered back.

"I have one more thing, I did not tell anyone. Sometime in the past Emma succeeded in sending people back. There is a message in my time, I think Emma in a cave in Yellow Stone Park, EM AEH Alive → EU," Marshal announced to the group.

"Why did you wait until now to tell me," Emma asked in a hurt voice, but her mind soared at the news.

She knew Adam, Eva and Hannah had made it through alive. A weight was lifted from her shoulders.

And she immediately recalled the biblical story of Adam and Eve. A warmth surged through her body.

Marshal confessed that he wanted to return to his time from the first day he arrived in the future. He was concerned that if Emma knew she had succeeded, she might stop the development of extraction and reinsertion. If she, did it would end his chance of returning to his own time.

"I am sure, Matt and Andrew are outcomes of your work. I am not sure where I fit other than being an accident or anomaly. Your DNA markers are probably not distinguishable because they may only exist on the woman's side. You got two males instead."

Marshal said as he gave a very surprised Emma another congratulation hug!

Also, I wanted a second successful reinsertion because I am not sure that Matt and Andrew are the products of your first success or of the success of the second reinsertion. Think about the odds of success and this intervention all from the same event.

Vesian had accepted the strange custom of giving a hug and she did so to say goodbye to Marshal.

She said that she wished there had never been a battle between the Caligrians and the people of Earth. She promised to continue her work to heal the relationship and to foster long term cooperation. Vesian thanked Marshal for taking the initiative to visit Caligria.

Marshal returned the kind comments and assured everyone in the room that the future was bright for the Caligrian-Earth partnership.

"Vesian, you will be remembered for the work you plan to do. I wish you the best in all your efforts," Marshal replied.

He gave a thumb up to Casperian and began the long fall forward in time.

After what seemed a long time, he saw the white light ahead. He hoped history had not changed too much and that his landing would be as gentle as last time.

Suddenly he was standing looking at Marial.

"How long have I been gone?" he asked Marial

"About ten minutes," Marial replied, "We guided you in as soon as we sensed the surge from Emma's time.

We were afraid to let you land too far into the future and of course we could not let you land even a few minutes into our past. We like your ten-minute rule."

"How long were you in the past?" Marial asked.

"I guess in all this coming and going I am the only one aging. I stayed almost a year here the first time I came, and I stayed back in Emma's and Vesian's time for almost two years after leaving here.

"When do you want to depart for your own time period?" Marial asked.

"The timing depends greatly on what your answer is to a very special request. I would like to learn about the lives of my two son's Matt and Andrew and take this information back with me to share with my wife. I will later ask to have my wife and daughter extracted at a point close to their deaths or whenever known history says it should be done. How long I stay here will be determined if this request can be accommodated. If it can, I would like to know what I must do to make it all happen smoothly," he replied.

Marial thought for a moment about this request. Now she understood why he was thought of as the prime anomaly in time travel principles. He was the exception to all the rules.

"The standard answer would be no, but I will need to take this up with the governing council. I will lobby for you, but I will tell you, everything you ask for is contrary to the guiding principles.

However, so far, your presence in the timeline has been contrary to all other planned events and it has always resulted in positive outcomes." Marial replied.

"Let's go to your quarters. I will link you into your family history. It has been very thoroughly studied and documented. You can read about your sons. I am sure you know they exist in our World-Wide Web, but we will not be able to let you meet at this time," Marial said as she led the way to the transport.

"I am allowed to give you access about your son's and their linage until the present, but you will not be able to access your own history. We just aren't sure how this would affect you or the history timeline," Marial continued, "I will check on your requests."

Marshal put on the wireless headset on to his head. He thought the topic of interest and he saw the material that was available. He could close his eyes since the vision was actually being formed in his mind. He had inquired about getting hard copies and was assured it was possible.

Marshal read about Matt and Andrew's families and their long history of contribution. Matt and Samantha had indeed settled in San Diego. Andrew and Alton had lived for most of their lives in the Loss Angelos area.

They all were very active and influential in the continued relationship with the Caligrians. Their work influenced the move of Earthlings into an active space exploration program. Not all subsequent family members were as productive or as influential as Matt and Andrew. There were even a few black sheep.

He looked up his daughter, Sabrina. He had already figured out that if he were able to learn of her family tree, he would also learn the answer to his request to extract them from the past. He was pleasantly surprised that he indeed found her present and mentioned in some articles with Matt and Andrew. This was even better than he had hoped. It became clear that from his time to the time extraction became possible, all of his family members were pulled forward. He now knew they were in the World Wide Web.

He received a cryptic message, "Congratulations from ALL the family. S"

He wondered who was breaking the rules and bet it was Samantha. She always had the urge to break the rules.

He then knew he could go home.

He printed out Matt's and Andrew's family tree, a few of their family pictures and some news reports about their accomplishments. He wanted just enough to convince their mother they indeed survived and prospered.

Marial returned with a mixed message.

"I am not allowed to tell you about the final resolution to your request. I do encourage you to return and be confident your wishes will get very careful consideration," Marial said as she broke her gaze with Marshal.

"I am fine with your answer. Thank you for your efforts," Marshal replied.

His own research assured him of the outcome he desired.

He then asked how precise his reinsertion into his time would be? He needed to know if it was in days, months, or years.

"Well, we are within seconds back to Emma's time. The farther we go back the less well we aim. We have about a three-month spread at the time of your extraction," Marial replied.

He wanted to return well before the extraction from Yellow Stone. He wondered if he could return with gold or any currency.

Marial simply said no but she could get him the stock market information for that time, and he could use that to generate some income.

He laughed as he shared the scene from a movie of hit his time. He laughed again when Marial asked what a movie was.

Marial pointed out that the pictures he was taking back was the most material they had ever transported back in time.

Marial went online and extracted the performance of six stocks that skyrocketed in the months preceding the extractions of Samantha, Matt, and Andrew.

He asked to be reinserted six months prior to Emma's Extraction of Samantha.

This would give him time to establish himself and be there when he, Matt and Andrew disappeared.

Marial handed him a pair of jeans and sports shirt. She also gave him a thermal coat and backpack that had several days of food.

This time Marial was the only one in the reinsertion room. He gave Marial a hug.

"I go back with great hope, confidence and enough material to write about that is well beyond my imagination. Thank you so much and I'll plan on catching up with you sometime in my future." he said quietly.

He stepped back to the focal point and felt a slight tingle and a momentary black out.

18 Yellow Stone

hen Marshal found himself standing almost at the same point on the trail in Yellow Stone where he had first departed.

He looked back along the trail. It was a crisp blustery morning. He was glad Marial had given him the jacket.

He hiked back down the trail toward the lodge and wondered when he had arrived. It felt like it was fall or early winter but there was no snow.

The newspaper at the lodge confirmed his guess. It was the seventh of October in the year prior to his extraction.

He bought a bus ticket to Jackson Hole, bought a Jackson Hole newspaper with the hundred-dollar bill Marial had surreptitiously passed to him in their last hug.

He wondered if there were now two bills with the identical serial numbers in the system.

At noon, he boarded the bus to Jackson Hole.

On the ride, he carefully scrutinized the want ads.

He was looking for a decent paying job but one where his references and background would not be scrutinized.

He found several leads.

One was at a welding/machine shop job. He was a very good welder and could read an engineering drawing with ease.

He got off the bus and asked directions to the address in the newspaper.

The bus did not go anywhere near the address and he did not want to spend his money on transportation, so he set out by foot. he was glad the city was not any larger then it was.

When he walked into the welding shop, he looked for the opportunity to immediately display his skill. He read the name tag of one of the welders and addressed him by name.

"John, let me help you with this. It appears the frame of this truck bed has cracked. Let me help you clean out the cracked area and then I'll fill it in," Marshal said as he grabbed some safety glasses and a rotary grinder.

John seemed surprised but did not stop him.

Marshal cut through the cracked area, cleaned the edges. He then proceeded to clamp on two metal beams with hydraulic clamps to hold the frame in perfect position. He made a few adjustments to insure everything was straight and true. Then he selected the appropriate welding rod, put on his welding shield, and laid in a perfect weld on the bottom half of the frame. He removed the support beams and finished the job.

"John, who in the hell is this guy," a person standing and watching asked.

"My name is Marshal and I need a job," he responded and extended his hand.

He noted the name tag read Elliot Reston, Supervisor.

Elliot did not shake his outstretched hand. Instead, he asked what he was doing out on the floor.

Marshal replied that he was responding to the ad in the paper and that he wanted to show what he could do rather than talk about what he could do.

"It is a dam good job and he sure the hell did it fast. About as good as I have seen," John said as he looked over the welding Marshal had done.

"Is this Henry Jone's truck?" Elliot said as he stepped forward to look at the weld.

"Sure is, we took the bed off to get to the frame," John replied.

"Take it for a spin. See if it runs without any problems. Then come to my office," Elliot instructed John.

"You come with me before some inspector tags me for having a non-employee out on the floor," Elliot said looking at Marshal.

"We pay twenty bucks an hour. You do what I tell you to do. You do it well, you get a ten percent bonus on the job. You mouth off to me and you go the same way as the jerk you are replacing. No coming in with alcohol on your breath.

No coming in late. No lollygagging around. Does that sound alright to you?" Elliot said as he looked him in the eyes.

"It's clear and simple enough for me," he said looking steadily back.

"We'll wait until John gets back but I already think I know what he will say. So welcome aboard," Elliot said and finally extended his hand.

"Thanks. I just got into town. I thought I would get the job first and then see about a convenient place to room. Do you have any suggestions?" Marshal asked.

"My sister, Emily runs a boarding house. The guy I fired use to live there. He wasn't too good here and he messed up his space there. She is trying to get it fixed up. Are you any good at spackling and painting? You might be able to get a month free rent for fixing up the room and bath," Elliot replied.

"Good as new. Couldn't have done better myself," John said when he came into the office.

"Take Marshal out with you and get the bed back on the truck. For once we will get done early with a job," Elliot said as he pointed to the door.

"I'll call my sister and let her know you are coming. I'll give you her address when you get done. It is walking distance from here," Elliot said in a loud voice.

"I never saw him hire someone so fast. We've been short-handed since he fired Dave. Dave wasn't very good, but he did do some work. Elliot and I have both been working overtime trying to keep our customers from getting too mad," John said as they walked back into the shop.

"Well, let's get caught up. I am willing to come in early tomorrow. Today, I need to get a place to sleep and some supplies so I can work." Marshal replied.

After getting the truck bed back on he went back to the office. He got directions and set off to meet Elliot's sister. He hoped the bedroom was in good enough shape to use immediately.

He decided that Emily could have been Elliot's twin. If she was, he figured she had gotten the short straw. She was pleasant and he immediately picked up on an inner strength you did not want to cross.

The room was clean. The bed came with two sets of sheets, two pillows, a blanket and bed cover.

It was clear the room walls needed cleaning, repairing, and painting.

The bathroom had been cleaned but he wanted to do it again.

"Do you have the cleaning supplies I can use to clean the bathroom again," he asked?

"Sure, I had the cleaning lady do it once already, but you're welcome to do it again. The cleaning supplies are in the mud room. You are welcome to use them anytime. Just let me know if something is getting low." she replied.

"Elliot said you were willing to clean, repair and paint. I'll let you have a free month rent if you do. My brother doesn't impress easily but you managed to impress him. I hope you work out.

I have two sets of keys. I will keep one set. You get the other. Please don't make spares. If you lose your keys just see me. Then we'll get some more made. The lock has been changed so no one but you and I have access.

I have four borders. Please be quiet after ten PM. Your key will open the front door and your room. You can come and go as you please.

There is a small frig in your room for snacks.

I do serve a simple breakfast. Since you are working at Elliot's place you will probably want breakfast at seven AM. However, I do serve it as early as six AM.

You are on your own during the week for lunch and dinner. On the weekends, I do prepare a brunch and an afternoon dinner.

Do you have any questions," she asked?

"Well, I need to get a few supplies; how do I get to the grocery, a reasonable clothes shop and a shoe shop?" he asked.

Emma gave him the address of the traditional shopping stores.

He left his humble abode after looking up the address for the Goodwill shop.

There he was able to get half a dozen sports shirts, seven work pants, two work shirts, a pair of work boots and a pair of dress shoes.

He also picked up an old but sharp kitchen knife, a couple of plates, coffee mugs and a coffee maker, a large thermos, and an old stainless steel lunch box.

All together this cost him fifty-three dollars.

He went to the grocery store and bought himself a half pound of salami, half a pound of ham, some cheddar cheese and a loaf of all grain bread, a large onion and two large tomatoes and a pound of coffee.

He stopped by the clothing store Emily told him about and bought a package of six under pants.

He had three dollars left in his pocket.

He figured he would be losing weight in the week ahead.

He returned to his room with his treasures.

He had found an iron and ironing board in his closet.

He sought out Emily and enquired about the laundry.

"Well, you will need to supply your own soap. I will let you have enough for what you need to wash tonight. How many loads do you have?" She inquired.

"Well, I would like to do two loads. I am going to be short until pay day. You can have Elliot hold what I owe you if that would make you feel better," he replied.

"No, if you get to cleaning and fixing up your room, we'll get along just fine," Emily responded.

Her friend at Goodwill had described Marshal to her and she watched what he brought in on the return from his shopping trip. He seemed to be a guy trying to get started on the right path and he was being frugal.

She would just keep an eye on him until she was sure he was OK.

Marshal did his laundry, cleaned the bathroom, and finished the evening getting his "new" clothes ironed and hung up.

He mused over his journey back to his time and the journey from battlefield commander against the Caligrians to local shop welder in Jackson Hole.

The next morning, he had his breakfast at six and was in the shop early.

He decided to put himself into the work in the shop.

Soon the shop was back on schedule on all the work.

His room got repaired and painted and he did some other maintenance work for Emily. They got along well, and she often invited him to evening dinner.

He preferred to eat in since he did not want to be too well known in the area.

Winter in Jackson Hole was one of either participating in winter sports or sitting in bars drinking. Many of the population did both.

He went skiing and ice fishing.

He was now invested in the market in the stocks he had been directed to by those in the future. He was doing very well and just a month he could have stopped working at the Elliot's welding shop. However, he knew he would be bored if he had too much time on his hands.

He bought himself a computer and went back to writing. In his mind it had been several years since he had last written anything. His recent experience provided him with a wealth of material. He could write the exact truth and it would seem like science fiction. He found the words flowed freely from his fingers. Every day he targeted three thousand words.

Work, the market, some skiing, ice fishing with John and writing consumed him and the time swiftly melted away.

He did not achieve three thousand words a day but did come in around two thousand words per day on average. He had seven novels stored in his computer by the end of June.

His worldly wealth had grown to exceed ten million dollars.

The future had given him the best stock tips one could have wanted!!

He let Elliot know he was planning to quit. Elliot tried to get him to stay.

He let Elliot know how grateful he was for having given him the job and promised to stay long enough to train his replacement, but that July thirty-first was his last day.

He thanked Emily for having taken such good care of him and that she would hear from him in the future.

By July 15 he was free from his job.

He went to the Oregon coast and checked in on Samantha's grandmother who was living in a nursing home. It was basic and well managed. There was nothing he could personally do. He arranged with the nursing home for an account to fund any support her grandmother would need.

He returned to Yellow Stone and went camping.

One night he went to the cave and removed the skull with the cryptic message to Emma. He cut out the section of skull with the message and put it in his backpack.

He would someday carry it to the future so it could be put into the museum of time travel.

He watched himself arrive with his family. It was great to see Nora after all the time that had passed for him. Nora looked as beautiful to him as the day he met her some forty years before. Matt and Andrew were joking or sparing with each other as always.

Two days later he followed Samantha out along the trail. He would lag well behind and let his other self-follow, Samantha. He watched as they both blinked out of existence and fell toward the future.

He jogged on and returned to the campsite he had set up until he could go as himself back to the lodge. How it was possible was beyond his understanding.

For a short period of time, this time had held two of him.

The next morning, he followed Matt and Andrew up along the same trail. He stayed well back so they would not be able to identify him. He watched as they blinked out at the same spot as he and Samantha had disappeared.

Once again, he returned to his campsite. He broke camp and returned to the hotel in the same outfit as he had left for his jog the day before.

"Where have you been? We called you in as a missing person, but they said they could not register you as missing for another twelve hours. Matt and Andrew have gone out looking for you," Nora said as she rushed forward and gave him a hug.

"You look somehow different," she remarked.

Marshal had decided to share the time travel story immediately. He knew it would take a few days for it to sink in and be believed.

He sat Nora down and let her know that he was going to tell her a story that would break her heart. It was a story that she would find hard to believe. It was a story she would need to accept. He told her that he had proof of what he was about to tell her.

"Have you gone over the edge?" Nora asked as she put her hand to his forehead.

"No, please sit down and look at these pictures. You will see Matt; with the young lady we all met the other night at dinner. She and I fell into the future yesterday. Matt and Andrew fell into the future today.

I returned from the future several months ago so I could be with you when you learned these facts.

Andrew meets someone in the future and falls in love with him. Again, please look at the pictures and the dates.

This all happened because if it didn't all three would die in a common car accident tomorrow. The people in the future chose to extract the three before the accident so they could get healthy DNA for a program to counteract the DNA decay in the future," Marshal explained as he gave her the pictures from the distant future.

"Where did you get these?" Nora said as she looked through the pictures he had brought back.

"These were in the historic archives some twenty thousand years in the future," Marshal replied.

"This is so hard to believe. I just saw both of the boys leave not less than thirty minutes ago," Nora said in a voice of concern.

"I am sorry to tell you we will not see them again for the rest of our lives in this time frame. I did some checking when I was in the future and I put in a request that you and the rest of the family eventually get pulled into the future.

Either Sabrina or Samantha sent me a cryptic message indicating we would all be together on the World Wide Web.

"Ok, if I buy into this story, when do I get to see Matt and Andrew again?" Nora asked.

"I only know that you will not be pulled forward until the time they feel you will not cause a disruption in history. The same will be true of Sabrina," Marshal replied

"Why did you come back," Nora asked?

"To be with you," Marshal said giving her a hug.

He had tears in his eyes.

He had his love in his arms and he had the future to look forward to.

THE END

About the Author

Ronald E. Mueller
www.remwriter95.net/

Ron has a fascination with the scientific thought process. He writes stories just beyond the possible but clearly achievable with just the right technological breakthrough. Ron's science fiction almost seems true. His heroes are not superhuman but rather the regular guy put into a must do situation.

These must do characters are of all genders and races. The bad guys are equally diverse.

Ron's background as a control system engineer and production system optimization has exposed him to how equipment is made. He is a professional engineer and has been around most of the developing technology of the day.

He was born in Brazil, grew up in Iowa, served in Vietnam, graduated from the University of South Florida, worked for Procter and Gamble for thirty-seven years and has been happily married for more than fifty years.

He is the father of three great offspring and now the grandfather of three really smart grandchildren.

He feels time overall has been good and that the journey he is on soars through fresh, invigorating environs. \

Books by the Author
Fiction Series

The Alex Evercrest Series
The River Front
The Girl on The Grill
Missing
Maggot
Racist
Votive Candles
Windy City
Country Road
Pool of Blood
Sins of the Daughter
Body Parts
The Skull Collector
The Vanishing
The Shadow Fighter
Moonshine
Grief's Trajectory
The Magic Touch
Northern Lights
Alex Evercrest Heroine
Alex Evercrest Collection Two
New Direction
A Family Affair
Disruption
Aftermath
The St. Lebuinnus Church Murder

A Brian O'Neil Novel
Hawaiian Phoenix
Moon Curser
Death Broker

The Problem Solver Series
Solutions
Drug Lords
Border Crosser
The Problem Solver Collection

The Taelo Series
The Early Years
The Golden Feather
Journey of Discovery
Dangerous Passage
Condor Clan Slingers
Circumvention
The Journey of Sages
Collection
Future Leaders Journey

A Taelo Story:
White Swan and Quiet Pheasant
The Child's Name
Floating Cloud
Quiet Rabbit
Busy Bee
Little Otter & Talking Wren
Broken Spear
Burley Bear & Meadow Flower
Taelo Story Collection

269

Science Fiction

The Savitar Series:
Journey's End
Savitar
Confluence
Savitar Series Collection

The Door Series
The Door
Aliens We
The Endless Hole
The Swarm
Esoteric Journey
The Gentle Eye
The Door Series Collection

Bram Nielson Series
The Fold
The Message
Fold Wormhole
Negative Fold
Ripples in Time
Bram Nielson Collection

Single Science Fiction Books:
The Future Awaits
The Event
Viajante 7
Star Mote Castle

Imagination by Courtney Huynh and Chloe Parker

Published by: Around the World Publishing LLC.

www.ingramcontent.com/pod-product-compliance
Lightning Source LLC
Chambersburg PA
CBHW070516100726
47907CB00004B/856